One Chance to Escape

David suddenly felt quite empty inside. He was sure that he would be unable to move when the time came. Then he saw before him the endless succession of days, months, and years in the concentration camp if he did not. David clenched his teeth so hard that he felt the muscles of his throat grow taut. Then he saw the signal.

Nineteen, twenty . . . the half minute would be up when he had counted slowly to thirty. . . . David set his foot in a gap higher up the barbed wire. . . .When would the searchlight come? They could not be certain of shooting him in the dark. . . .

I Am
David

I Am
David

Anne Holm

Translated from the Danish by
L. W. KINGSLAND

Harcourt, Inc.
Orlando Austin New York San Diego Toronto London

For information about permission to reproduce selections from this book,
write to Permissions, Houghton Mifflin Harcourt Publishing Company,
215 Park Avenue South, New York, New York 10003.

www.hmhco.com

First U.S. edition 1965

Library of Congress Cataloging-in-Publication Data
Holm, Anne, 1922–
[David. English]
I am David/Anne Holm: translated from the Danish by L. W. Kingsland.
p. cm.
Previously published under title: North to freedom.
Summary: After escaping from an Eastern European concentration camp where he
has spent most of his life, a twelve-year-old boy struggles to cope with an entirely
strange world as he flees northward to freedom in Denmark.
[1. Refugees—Fiction.] I. Kingsland, L.W. II. Title.
PZ7.H7322Iae 2004
[Fic]—dc22 2003057006
ISBN-13: 978-0-15-205161-7 ISBN-10: 0-15-205161-9
ISBN-13: 978-0-15-205160-0 (pb) ISBN-10: 0-15-205160-0 (pb)

DOC 20 19
4500525946

Printed in the United States of America

I Am
David

1

David lay quite still in the darkness, listening to the men's low muttering. But this evening he was aware of their voices only as a vague, meaningless noise in the distance, and he paid no attention to what they were saying.

"You must get away tonight," the man had told him. "Stay awake so that you're ready just before the guard's changed. When you see me strike a match, the current will be cut off and you can climb over—you'll have half a minute for it, no more."

In his mind's eye David saw once again the gray, bare room he knew so well. He saw the man and was conscious, somewhere in the pit of his stomach, of the hard knot of hate he always felt whenever he saw him. The man's eyes were small, repulsive, light in color, their expression never changing; his face was gross and fat, yet at the same time square and angular. David had known him all his life, but he never spoke to him more than was necessary to answer his questions; and though he had known his name for as long as he could remember, he never said anything but "the man" when he spoke about him or thought of him. Giving him a name would be like admitting that he knew him; it would place him on an equal footing with the others.

But that evening he had spoken to him. He had said, "And if I don't escape?"

The man had shrugged his shoulders. "That'll be none of my business. I have to leave here tomorrow, and whatever my successor may decide to do about you, I shan't be able to interfere. But you'll soon be a big lad, and there's need in a good many places for those strong enough to work. Of course he may think that you aren't yet big enough but that it's still worthwhile feeding you here."

David knew only too well that those other places would not be any better than the camp where he now was. "And if I get away without being caught, what then?" he had asked.

"Just by the big tree in the thicket that lies on the road out to the mines, you'll find a bottle of water and a compass. Follow the compass southward till you get to Salonika, and then when no one's looking, go on board a ship and hide. You'll have to stay hidden while the ship's at sea, and you'll need the

2

water then. Find a ship that's bound for Italy, and when you get there, go north till you come to a country called Denmark—you'll be safe there."

David had very nearly shown his astonishment, but he had controlled himself and, hiding his feelings, had merely said, "I don't know what a compass is."

The man had shown him one, telling him that the four letters indicated the four main points and that the needle, which was free to move, always pointed in the same direction. Then he had added, "The half minute the current's cut off is intended for you. If you try to take anyone with you, you can be sure that neither of you will get away. And now clear off before you're missed."

David did not know what had possessed him to say it. He had never asked the man for anything, partly because he knew it would be of no use, but chiefly because he would not—when you hated someone, you did not ask him for anything. But tonight he had done it: when he had reached the door, he had turned around and, looking straight into that coarse, heavy face, had said, "I'd like a piece of soap."

For a moment there had been complete silence in that bare, gray room. The man looked as if he were going to say something, but he did not, all the same. Instead, he picked up a cake of soap that lay by the side of the washbasin in the corner and threw it on the table. All he said was, "Now go."

So David had gone, as quickly as it was possible to go without appearing to be in a hurry.

The men's muttering was fainter now—some of them must have fallen asleep. The camp's latest arrival was still talking—David recognized his voice because it was less flat and grating than the others'. Whenever the newcomer dozed off to sleep, he was seized with a nightmare, and then they would all wake up again. The night before, this had happened just before the guard was changed, but if he took longer to fall asleep this evening, then it might be possible for David to slip out before the others were awakened again.

David was not yet sure whether he would make the attempt. He tried to figure out why the man had told him to do it. It was certainly a trap: just as he was climbing over, the searchlight would suddenly swing around and catch him in its beam, and then they would shoot. Perhaps something pleasant was going to happen tomorrow, and the man wanted him shot first. David had always known that the man hated him, just as much as David hated *him* in return. On the other hand, nothing pleasant had ever yet happened in the camp that David could remember, and he was now twelve years old—it said so on his identity card.

And then quite suddenly David decided he would do it. He had turned it over in his mind until his head was in a whirl, and he still could not understand why the man had told him to escape. David had no wish to make the attempt: it would only be a question of time before he was caught. But suppose it were a trap and they shot him—it would all be over quickly anyway. If you were fired at while trying to escape, you would be dead within a minute. Yes, David decided to try.

There could not be many minutes left now. Over in the guardroom he could hear the men moving about and getting dressed, and he could hear the guard yawning as his pace grew slower. Then came the sound of new steps, and David pressed himself even more closely against the wall. It was the man: the faint, sleepy yellow light from the guardroom shone for a moment on his face as he passed the window. He went up to the guard, and David suddenly felt quite empty inside. He was sure that he would be unable to move when the time came. Then he saw before him the endless succession of days, months, and years that would pass if he did not. The waiting would kill him in the end, but it might take a long time: unless you were old, it might take years, as he had seen with all of them. And it would grow worse and worse, all the time; David clenched his teeth so hard that he felt the muscles of his throat grow taut. Then the man struck a match.

Nineteen, twenty . . . the half minute would be up when he had counted slowly to thirty . . . David set his foot in a gap higher up the barbed wire . . . When would the searchlight come? They could not be certain of hitting him in the dark . . . and if they did not hurry, he would be over.

A moment later he had touched the ground on the other side, and as he ran, he said angrily to himself, "What a fool you are! There's plenty of ground to cover yet—all this great flat stretch without so much as the stump of a tree for shelter. They'll wait till you've nearly reached the thicket . . . they'll think it more amusing if you believe you've almost gotten to safety."

Why didn't they hurry up? The thought pounded through his head as every moment he expected to see the ground lit up in front of him. Then he stopped. He would run no more. When the beam of light caught him, they should see him walking away quite calmly. Then they would not enjoy it so much; they would feel cheated. The thought filled David with triumph.

When he was little, it had been his most burning desire to get the better of them, especially of the man. And now he would! They would be forced to shoot him at the very moment when he was walking quietly away and taking no notice of them!

David was so taken up with his victory over them that he had gone a dozen yards past the spot where the thicket hid him from the camp before he realized that no one had fired. He stopped short. What could have happened? He turned, found a place where the thicket was thin enough to peer through, and looked across at the low buildings outlined against the dark sky, like an even darker smudge of blackness. He could faintly hear the tread of the guard, but it came no nearer and sounded no different from usual, only farther off. Nothing at all appeared different; there was no sign of anything afoot.

David frowned in the darkness and stood for a moment undecided; it couldn't possibly . . . ? He trotted on, following the edge of the thicket toward the big tree, running faster the nearer he got, and when he reached the tree, he threw himself down on the ground, searching frantically around the trunk with his hands.

There was the bundle. David leaned up against the tree shivering with cold, although it was not cold at all. The bundle was a piece of cloth wrapped around something and tied in a knot. He fumbled with the knot, but his fingers were clumsy and would not respond—and then he suddenly realized that he dared not undo it. There would be something dangerous inside the bundle . . . He tried to gather his thoughts together sufficiently to think what it might be, but his imagination did not get beyond a bomb.

It would make little difference, he thought desperately—a bullet or a bomb—it would soon be over, either way. Frantically, his fingers awkward, he struggled with the cloth.

But there was no bomb in the cloth. It was a square handkerchief tied crosswise over a bottle of water and a compass, just as the man had said.

The thought now occurred to David for the first time that he might simply have walked past the bundle. He was quite alone: nobody was there to make him pick it up . . . He barely managed to turn aside before he was sick.

Afterward he felt carefully all around the square-shaped bundle. A bottle, a compass—there was something else. David's eyes had grown accustomed to the darkness; in the bundle there were also a box of matches, a large loaf of bread, and a pocketknife.

So the man had intended him to escape after all! He would send out a search party in the morning, but not before . . . The night was his, and it was up to him to make the most of it.

All this had taken only a few minutes, but to David it felt like hours. His hand closed tightly around the soap—he had not let go of it for a moment since he first got it. He recalled the hours he had spent that evening lying on his plank bed listening to the muttered conversation of the men and thinking over what the man had said. He remembered, too, that it would be only a matter of time before he was caught again; but that, like everything else, no longer seemed important. All that mattered now were his bundle and the freedom of the night that lay ahead. Slowly he tucked the piece of soap into a corner of the handkerchief, laid the bottle, bread, and knife on top, tied the ends together, took a firm grip on the knot, and looked at the compass in his hand.

Then he ran.

When he looked back afterward, all he could recall of the five days that followed was running and look-ing all the time at the compass to make sure he was traveling in the right direction. Every night he ran, and he ran all night long. Once he slipped into a water hole, and the mud caked on him as it dried. Once he was so torn by branches that blood oozed from the scratches on his face, hands, and legs. He would never forget that night. He had come to a close thicket of thornbushes, and the needle indicated that he should go straight through it. He had hesitated a moment and then tried running a few yards along the edge of it, but the compass needle immediately swung around. Perhaps he could have recovered his direction a bit farther on, but he knew so little about compasses that he dared not risk it. And so he plunged into the thicket, elbows up to protect his face. The first branch that struck him hurt painfully, and so did the first gash along his arm, but after that he noticed nothing and just crashed his way through. The nights were usually completely quiet, but that night he could hear a whimpering moan the whole time. Not until afterward did he realize that the sound had come from himself.

He ran all the time, sometimes fairly slowly so that it took him hours to go a short way, sometimes so quickly that he felt his blood pounding. Every morning with the first glimmer of daylight he lay down to sleep. It was not very difficult to find somewhere to sleep in that sparsely inhabited district. David had no idea what the countryside looked like; for him it was only a place where he must run through the night and hide by day.

Two other incidents remained in his memory: they were moments when fear grew to a sharp-pointed terror that seemed to pierce him right through. The first one happened just as it was growing dark one evening. David was awakened by something warm and hairy touching his hand. He lay still, tense with fear . . . It was some minutes before he could bring himself to turn his head, and then he saw—a sheep.

But it spelled danger, nevertheless, for where there are sheep, there must also be people not far away, and that evening David did not stop to recover his breath for some hours afterward.

Yet he was glad enough to come across more sheep later that night. David was used to hard work and satisfied with very little food, and he had been as sparing as he could with the bread and water, but after two whole days the bottle was empty and the bread eaten. He could manage without bread, but it was dreadful to be so thirsty. In the end he could think of hardly anything but water, but where was he to get it?

At that point he almost stumbled over two shepherds who lay asleep on the ground wrapped in their cloaks. His heart, which had been thumping so loudly all through the night, missed a beat, so terror-stricken was he. But he stopped himself just in time; bare feet make no noise and the two men had heard nothing.

David was about to step back, slowly and cautiously, when he caught sight, in the moonlight, of a bucket with a lid and the embers of a burned-down fire. Food! And where there was food, there was probably water, too!

That night David went no farther. He kept watch till daybreak, far enough off to give him a chance to escape should that prove necessary, and yet near enough to be back in a moment as soon as the two shepherds were out of sight in the morning. There was little doubt that this was their regular camping place for the night, for they left their bundles and the bucket behind. Perhaps they would soon be back, but that was a risk David decided he must take. Without food, or at least without water, he would not be able to last many more hours. He was familiar enough, from his experiences in the camp, with what happened when a man was left without food and water.

What had nearly proved a catastrophe ended as a stroke of good fortune. There was some soup left in the bucket, and in one of the bundles he found a chunk of bread. He broke the bread unevenly, leaving a small piece behind. Then he filled his bottle with soup. He replaced the lid and knocked it off again with his elbow. He did not know whether sheep ate bread and soup, but if they did, he wanted to make it look as if they had been there.

After that night he took care to run at a more even pace and to stop more often, but for shorter periods, to recover his breath. He must not again risk being so tired that he saw nothing and stumbled on blindly.

David edged cautiously forward on his stomach. It was the second time he had found himself close to a town, and for the second time the compass was directing him to cross a main road. He dared not disobey it; it was almost as if some part of the man himself were traveling with him.

He ought to have asked how long it would take him to reach Salonika; he had only two mouthfuls of soup left now and a single bite of bread.

And there were people about. That meant he had not nearly so much of the night at his disposal—he would have to wait until they had gone to bed. He told himself that he should have known all along he would occasionally come across towns . . . He forced himself to lie absolutely still. But he was not sleepy any longer, and when he was not sleepy, lying still became almost unbearable, for then it was difficult not to think—and David knew that he must not think. He had learned that—then. The only thing to do was to take no notice; you could look and listen, but you must not let what you heard or saw penetrate your thoughts. You must not let your thoughts dwell upon anything more important than whether it would rain or turn out fine, whether you had long to wait for your next meal, or when the guard would be changed. And you must not be too interested in those things either—you must merely make use of them to fill your thoughts and prevent other things from slipping into your mind.

Since the evening of his escape, the things he had formerly occupied his thoughts with were no longer there; but others had taken their place— hurrying along as fast as possible during the night, stopping as soon as the darkness began to lift so that he could find a good hiding place before day broke, looking after his bundle and avoiding the temptation of taking an extra bite or another drop to drink, going in the right direction all the time so that the compass needle did not shift its position. These things served to fill his thoughts to the exclusion of other matters. But when it came to lying still and yet being wide awake—that was dangerous! So he began to think about a feeling he had had several times during the previous night—that the ground he was traveling over was changing, becoming more up and down . . . that mountains would bar the road to Salonika.

Don't think, don't think! David clenched his

hands, gripping a tuft of grass. He mustn't think at all, for if he did, there was only one thing to think about—that he would not be able to run any farther, that he would have to wait far too long before he was captured. Why had they not caught him the night he crossed the bridge? He could not swim, and so the bridge had been his only way over the river, and he had been quite sure he would be caught there. Yes, that had been the only restful moment in all those long days and nights—crossing that bridge and feeling certain they would catch him.

But no one had come.

David's feet were no longer part of him. When he himself cared no more, his feet followed their own path independently, stealing along noiselessly, surely, guiding his body so that he kept to the shadows and avoided obstacles, stopping him in time or urging him on whenever he felt he would rather lie down and wait till he was caught.

And his feet had carried him over the bridge.

He clenched his teeth. "Salonika!" he whispered and went on repeating the word over and over again to himself until it seemed to fill his brain. "Go south till you reach Salonika. Think of nothing else yet!"

At that moment the sound of a car pulling up caused him to stiffen. Was he far enough from the road?

Then he heard voices—he was so terrified that he nearly jumped out of his skin. He was quite unused to the sound of voices by this time; the last he had heard were the guard's and the man's.

But these were different, and they were coming nearer! David relaxed completely so that he would make as little noise as possible, and as he did so, he thought that in a moment all would be over—everything.

The men sat down a little way off and lit cigarettes, and it gradually dawned upon David that they were not looking for him at all. He began to listen to what they were saying. He found it difficult to follow them since their speech differed from the man's, but after a while David was able to distinguish words that were familiar to him.

They drove a delivery truck, like the men who brought supplies to the camp, where no one stopped them or interfered with them. They were arguing now but with no great heat; one of them wanted to drive on, and the other wanted to visit someone first in the town David had seen nearby. In the end he got his way; the first man said he would go with him, but only for half an hour as it was a long way home.

Like an echo of his own thoughts, David caught the word "Salonika!"

The next thing he was fully aware of was that he was sitting in the truck as it began to move off.

The men had driven toward the town, and David had allowed his feet to carry him mechanically after the truck. It had stopped on the outskirts of the town, and when the two men had disappeared into a house, David's feet had gathered speed until he reached it.

And now he had a lift! There had been lights in the houses, but no one had seen him. The truck door had not been locked, and although the back of the truck was well filled with packing cases, there was room enough for David to squeeze down between two of them and squat on the floor. And now he was on his way . . . It was pitch dark inside, both because it was nighttime and because the packing cases covered the little window in the partition that separated the back of the truck from the cab where the men were sitting. And even if they opened the door from the outside, they would not be able to see David without moving all the packing cases. It was a strange feeling, sitting quite still and being carried along. David had seen cars and trucks, but he had never ridden in one, nor in any other kind of vehicle, and just as it occurred to him that he had no idea how he was going to get out again, he began to feel sleepy—dreadfully sleepy. He strove to keep awake as long as he could, but the even purr of the engine and the swaying and jolting of the truck proved too much. He was asleep.

He had no idea how long he slept. He woke because the engine sounded different, as if it were starting up. But surely it could not have been very long? He had lost the habit of sleeping at night. With infinite care, in almost imperceptibly small jerks, he pushed aside the packing case nearest the cab where the men were sitting, and he had soon made a narrow opening through which, when he put one eye to it, he could see a strip of the little window. No, it was still night: it was dark where the men were sitting, too.

If he could only get out before it was day, before they opened the truck and found him . . .

He suddenly knew what it felt like to be in one of the cells they had talked about in the camp—locked in, doubled up in inky blackness without being able to move, without being able to die.

"Johannes!" he whispered. "Johannes . . ."

For three whole winters and summers, ever since he was small, he had known that he must not allow himself to think, and above all that he must never think about Johannes. And now he had done it.

David let his head sink upon his chest and tried

to fight against the flood of memory that poured over him, the terror, the hatred, the frightening questions that burned like fire within him. And through it all, Johannes . . . Johannes smiling; Johannes who, even if his voice had grown lifeless and grating like the others', had never changed inside himself; Johannes to whom you could say anything; and Johannes who at last had fallen to the ground and remained lying there—and was dead.

Never since that day had David thought about him. That night, when they were all in bed, he had gone out into the yard and looked at the spot where Johannes had fallen. He had been standing there for a long time when the man had come along and seen him.

"He died of a heart attack," he said. "Clear off now and get to bed!"

Since that day David had tried to think of nothing but mealtimes and the changing of the guard. At first it had made him ill, but later he had grown used to it. Why should it have come back to him just at this moment when all that mattered was getting to Salonika?

The voice came from somewhere far away. "I'm going with you to Salonika." David was not even sure it was Johannes' voice, so far away did it sound; but he knew it must have been because he suddenly felt exactly as he had when he was small and Johannes was with him.

"Thank you," he whispered.

And after that it was easy. He found a packing case that had not been properly nailed down. It contained some kind of food, round and firm, that tasted like a bit of cheese David had once had in the camp. He cut off a piece with his knife, as big a piece as he could get into his handkerchief. The men stopped the truck while it was still dark and left it without opening the door at the back. So David jumped out and found himself in the middle of a large town, and being careful to walk in the shadow of the houses—for there was no call to be foolhardy even if Johannes were with him—he had no difficulty in finding the harbor where the ships lay. There was a water faucet on the way, too. David watched a man turn it on and drink, and when he had gone and the street was quiet again, David was able to walk over to it and fill his bottle.

The ship he was to find needed no searching for either; it lay right in front of him, and on its stern he saw the word "Italy" painted in large white letters. And it was made fast to the quayside with a great thick rope, ready for David to climb up as soon as the man on watch had gone to the other end of the ship. All David needed to do was to find a length of twine with which to tie his bundle about his waist while he was climbing. The watchman did not hear him, no one heard him, and down in the bottom of the ship there was a great dark room filled with so many packing cases that he could barely squeeze himself in.

At first David was anxious to discover if there were any windows down there, but then he realized that he was now below the waterline and so of course there weren't any . . . The time had now come for him to open the last of his treasures, his box of matches.

He took care to shield the flame with his hands as he had often seen the camp guards do . . . and to use no more than one or two matches since he must be sparing with them.

He saw case after case, stacked right up to the deck above . . . and there were sacks as well. He found a corner where there were only a couple of sacks, and there he could stay well hidden even if someone came into the hold. But that was hardly likely to happen—not before they reached Italy. The sacks and cases were all clearly bound for Italy . . . Just as the second match died out, David caught sight of a large half-filled bottle standing on the edge of a case. He put his bundle down on the sacks, stretched on tiptoe to reach it, uncorked it, and thrust his finger inside the neck. He sniffed his finger cautiously. It smelled a little strong but not unpleasant—perhaps he could drink it. David took the bottle down and settled himself comfortably on his sacks. It would be a good thing to have if he were to be at sea for any length of time.

The noise of the engines woke David, but not until the ship was well underway did he lose the strange dreamlike sensation that had been with him ever since the moment in the truck when he had suddenly recalled Johannes. Then he knew what had happened. Sitting bolt upright on his sack, his eyes at first wide open and then closed in the darkness, he knew that Johannes was no longer with him— he had stayed behind in Salonika!

David struggled with all his might against the fear that grew within him . . . He told himself over and over again, "He promised nothing more: he only said he would stay with me till we got to Salonika."

But it did not help. All the coldness and dark-ness and infinite loneliness of the world filled David's mind until it seemed ready to burst. Then he knew no more.

And so the days passed. David lost count of them, for it was dark all the time and there was nothing to distinguish day from night. Once when he woke, he picked up the strange bottle by mistake for his own, and after that he took a drink from it every time staying awake any longer grew too much for him, for he discovered that drinking from it very soon made him feel sleepy. It tasted good, too—a little strong perhaps but not unpleasant—and then he could sleep a while longer.

Sometimes he told himself that he had only to scramble over to the door, open it, and go up the steps till he met someone—and all his troubles would be over. He wished desperately that he could put an end to his existence . . . but his feet would not budge, his legs refused to carry him the little distance he had to go before he could give himself up. He wanted to do it—but his body would not take him.

When at last he was discovered, he was taken completely by surprise. He woke up to hear a voice just above his head saying, "*Mamma mia*, what are you doing here?"

David jumped up like lightning but made no attempt to run. The man had very black hair, like all Italians. "Nothing," answered David in Italian.

The sailor opened his mouth to shout—but thought better of it and instead scrambled over to the door and shut it. Then he came back. He was not sure why he did this. Perhaps because the boy was so quiet—a very thin, very dirty boy who stood as still as death and who had the calmest face he had ever seen.

He ought to call someone and get the boy hauled up into the daylight. Then, by the beam of his flashlight, he looked down into the boy's strange dark eyes and knew he could not because that was just what those eyes expected him to do. The Italian sailor tried to shake off the feeling that the boy was going to die. His grandmother's eyes had looked like that the day before she died. But he might be wrong, of course; for one thing, his grandmother's eyes had been brown and this boy's were—well, it was not easy to see in that dim light—very dark gray, perhaps, or green.

So he said the first thing that entered his head. "Have you been drinking my wine?"

"Yes. I'd no more water in my bottle. I didn't know it was wine. Thank you."

The Italian shook his curly black head. Never had he met such a child! "First he swigs my wine without knowing what it is, and then he thanks me for it as if it weren't sheer robbery . . . !" And he was so quiet. A boy caught when he was up to mischief usually made off as fast as his legs would carry him . . . turned and twisted and looked all around for a way of escape—he did not just stand still and look you in the face!

"Where did you think you'd get to?" he asked helplessly.

"To Italy."

"Hm. Well, I suppose I shall have to hand you over to the captain . . ."

But the Italian knew very well that he would not be able to. "I don't think you're all there," he said. He dared not lay hands on him; he could not bring himself to do it. "On the other hand, we shall be in Salerno this evening. It's hardly worth the trouble dragging you along to the captain and having all the fuss . . . You can jump overboard just before we get in, and then I shan't have had anything to do with it . . . I'll see about getting you out of here."

"I can't swim," the boy said quietly.

"*Mamma mia!* Then you *aren't* all there! I won't have anything to do with it . . . I'll give you a lifebelt, and you must try to drift ashore . . ."

"Thank you."

The Italian went his way shaking his head.

David slept no more. He was hungry—but then he had been hungry the last four times he had awakened—and he had run out of food. That was a remarkable man. It was really very kind of him not to let the captain arrest him; he obviously did not know David was so tired that he could hardly hold out any longer. And now he must take to the water! He did not know anything about lifebelts, but the Italian seemed to think he could drift ashore in one. So perhaps he would run on his way for yet another night, perhaps several nights, before they finally caught up with him.

But although David felt certain he knew what the end would be, his body set about getting him ready. Automatically he stuffed his ragged shirt into his no less ragged trousers, tied his bundle securely, and sat down to wait.

It was some time before the man returned. When he did come, David made no move. Perhaps the sailor had had second thoughts about the lifebelt . . . but David was beyond caring.

The Italian had brought the lifebelt, however, and a piece of bread as well. David ate half of it on the spot while the man was showing him how to use his arms to make sure he drifted in the right direction. David watched and realized he would be almost up to his neck in water. He frowned—the talk about direction had put him in mind of his compass . . . Suppose getting wet were bad for it? He had better tie his bundle around his neck.

The man lowered him over the side of the ship on the end of a rope and told him not to splash about in the water until the ship was some way off; otherwise, he might be heard. The water was not particularly cold. David looked back at the ship as it sailed swiftly on. For a moment he thought he was going to drown . . . It might very well be an easy way of sending people to their death, a belt like that . . . It looked like a car tire, he thought. But he did not drown, and he found it was not even necessary to fling his arms about as he had been told to do, for the ship had created a strong wash that drove him nearer and nearer to the dark line of the coast.

But before long David realized it was not quite so easy . . . Several hours passed before he touched land, and by that time he was so cold that it might have been the depth of winter and so exhausted that he was quite incapable of feeling; only his feet had the will to carry him farther.

David stumbled, staggered, crawled, onward in the darkness, uphill all the time, the going hard and stony; it must be a mountain slope . . . Then he came to a road and staggered across it without even remembering to see if there were people about . . . then farther uphill until he came to cultivated land where something was growing in low straight lines . . . then another stretch of mountainside with hard sharp-edged stones that hurt his feet. And then he could go no farther.

But there was no one to disturb his sleep that

night, and when he woke, he was no longer tired. He was not even cold—he was pleasantly warm, in fact. He lay awake for a while with his eyes shut, basking in the warmth of his own body while he listened as usual for sounds about him. But all was quiet. Then opening his eyes, he sat up and looked.

David was not used to bright color: he was familiar only with various tones of gray and brown, and, of course, the blue of the sky. Well, yes, he had once seen a little red flower that had strayed inside the camp wall. Apart from that, color was something he had only heard of: he had seen only a pale and muddied reflection of it—in the ugliness of the camp and the equally ugly quarters of the guards.

He did not know how long he stayed there on the mountainside, sitting motionless, just gazing . . . Only when everything grew strangely misty did he discover that he was crying.

Far below him lay the sea, a sea bluer than any sky he had ever seen. The land curved in and out along its edge: in and out, up and down, all green and golden, with here and there the red of flowers too far off to be clearly seen. Down by the sea a road ran along the foot of the mountain, and near it lay occasional villages whose bright colors were dazzling . . . There were trees with many changing tints of green, and over it all shone the warming sun—not white-hot and spiteful and scorching, as the sun had shone upon the camp in the summer-time, but with a warm golden loveliness.

Beauty. David had once heard Johannes use the word. It must have been something like this he meant . . . Perhaps that was why he had come back and gone with him to Salonika, so that he, David, could sail across the sea till he came to a land of beauty.

His tears continued to flow, faster and faster, and he brushed them angrily away so that the mist before his eyes should not veil that beauty from him.

Suddenly he knew that he did not want to die.

He did not want to be caught; he did not want to die. His legs had carried him to the place where the truck stood waiting, and when the weight of loneliness had grown too much for him, Johannes had kept him company to Salonika. The strange man with the black head of hair had helped him to reach land with a lifebelt. An now that he had come to this place of beauty, he no longer wanted to die— he wanted to live . . .

2

For a long time David continued to sit and gaze upon the lovely scenery that lay before him. He knew he had much to do, but just then he was too preoccupied to think about it; his resolve to go on living seemed to have pushed everything else out of his mind. And he could not take his eyes off what he was looking at . . . Surely this was what one had eyes for—not for the ugly dark gray, oppressive buildings of the camp or the endless flat, bare ground that stretched away, dull brown and empty, as far as eye could reach . . . One had eyes to gaze on beauty, and David looked again and again upon the blueness of the sea, upon the coastline curving along its shore. He saw the bright colors of the landscape, its variegated greens intermingled with gold and red, fade into one another toward the horizon until everything melted into the blue of sea and sky far away over the mountains.

David looked down at his own hand lying in the grass and knew at once what he was going to do first. The grass was green, although summer was far advanced, so there must be water not very far away.

He looked first at the sun, then at his compass, and then at the sun again; it was very early—he still had a good hour before he need find a hiding place for the day. He took hold of his bundle and jumped up. And there was water—a lazy little runnel glinting in the sunlight in the midst of a much wider riverbed, which wound among trees and bushes where he could hide if anyone came along. David had his clothes off in no time; he had only a shirt and a pair of trousers kept up with string that the night's soaking had made remarkably stiff. He laid his trousers in the water and put a stone on top to prevent them from floating away. Then he soaked his shirt thoroughly and opened his bundle.

He stood there a moment, soap in hand. Sometimes when they first arrived in camp, they were quite white and clean all over with no smell about them . . . He hardly dared try—then he made an attempt, beginning with his hands.

It worked . . . almost. David scrubbed away until he was in a sweat; he picked up his shirt to rub himself with, and then he got on much better. He had thought dirt was much more difficult to get off.

Then he remembered the sea; being wet through all night must have helped considerably. His head was a bit of a problem, but David would not give up; he was going to get all that dirt off, all that reminded him of the camp and smelled of its inmates. He lay right down, dipping his head in the water so that his hair was thoroughly wet, rubbed soap all over it until his arms grew tired, then ducked again and rubbed away with his shirt until his hair no longer felt sticky. He turned cold, but he took no notice; his one thought was to be quite, quite clean. His shirt gradually took on a brighter color, and then he set about his trousers as well. They, too, became brighter. Finally he sat down with his knife and whittled away at a twig until he had a sharp point of clean wood. He pricked himself a couple of times in the process, but in the end his nails were clean, toenails included.

The sun glistened on a drop of water as it fell from his hand to his knee. David wiped it off, but it left no tidemark: there was no more dirt to rub away. He took a deep breath and shivered. He was David. Everything else was washed away, the camp, its smell, its touch—and now he was David, his own master, free—free as long as he could remain so.

David took a look around—it would not do to go on sitting where he was; a little higher up the hill he caught sight of a house among the trees, and a little farther down lay the road. There would soon be people about, and he must first find a safe hiding place.

He followed the stream a little way, then turned off and went straight down toward the coast. The going was steep, but David's tough-skinned feet were used to finding places where he could get a good foothold. His body was lithe and quick, and he found no difficulty in keeping his balance. Just before he came to the road, he stopped irresolutely; he *could* hide in the undergrowth down there. But that meant he would have to lie flat all day, and when he was not sleeping, it would be very irksome to lie in roughly the same position all the time. Now that he was close to the road, he could see that there were houses at regular intervals along both sides of it— not right on it but a little above or below with gates leading onto it. Beautiful houses, pink and pale yellow and white, with gaily painted doors and green trees and climbing plants growing on their walls. But for that very reason they spelled danger—where there were houses, there were people.

A little farther on, the ground fell away so steeply from the road that there were no houses for some distance—it looked as if he would have to cross over.

His heart began to beat quickly. The road wound among the hills, and you could not see much of it at a time because it kept bending sharply around the spurs. Even if he were certain the road was clear at the moment, someone might come along just as he began to cross. Not cars nor people walking on the hard surface, for David's hearing was good, but if anyone were walking on the grass verge, he would not be able to hear him until he was right on top of him. Was it all to last only a single morning, his beautiful surroundings, his desire to live? Was it all to be taken from him again by a single stranger coming along, now or in half an hour's time?

But if he stayed where he was, his danger would be just as great. Among the trees something was growing low on the ground in long rows; it must have been planted there to grow in such straight lines, and someone might come along to tend it. Something brightly colored, not yellow nor red but orange, caught his eye in the green grass—it was round and rather soft. David picked it up without thinking and walked the last few yards to the road.

The morning was still young, and everywhere it was quiet in the sunlight; there was no one to be seen . . . there was only the stranger David knew might be coming along just around the nearest spur of rock.

He crossed the road, not slowly nor hurriedly. Afterward, when his heart had stopped beating so fast, he realized that his decision had changed everything. Ever since the night he had found the bundle lying under the tree as the man had told him it would be, his feet had carried him along, deciding the way for him.

This time it was he who had made the decision. His feet had not wanted to take the risk of crossing the road, and he had mastered them and forced them to do it. The thought gave David a warm feeling of strength and freedom. From now on he would think for himself and make his own decisions, and his feet and hands and body would be his servants to do his bidding.

Down right by the edge of the water he would be sheltered from the road, and the nearest house was some way off. David did not think anyone would be able to see him from there, but he was not sure—and it was necessary to be sure. Over on the next headland, he could see a kind of cave. If he could get over there, he would be safe for the day. But there was a narrow ravine between him and the cave, and it was too far for him to jump across. David put his bundle down and stretched his leg over the edge, feeling about with his foot for some support; but it was very steep and slippery. Only a yard separated him from the best hiding place he had ever seen!

I will *get over!* he said to himself. It must be possible—there must be some way . . . Perhaps he could find a big stone and drop it into the cleft so that he could clamber across? But struggle as he would, he could not budge the only boulder that looked big enough. He would not give in, however, until he finally realized that he could not move it and was only wasting his strength to no purpose. If he had a rope . . . but there was nothing he could make it fast to on the other side, and the only thing he had that at all resembled a rope was the bit of string around his trousers.

Then something brown caught his eye a little farther down on his own side of the ravine. A wooden packing case—or rather a plank from one.

David suppressed his excitement. It was not big enough, he told himself; of course it would not be big enough. But he ought to try, just to make sure. When his heart was beating normally again, he set off after it. The plank was long enough! He could lay it across like a bridge, and he could pull it in after he had crossed over it so that no one could follow him!

But was it stout enough? He found two small

stones and laid them one under each end of the plank; then he stepped carefully onto it. It creaked a little, but it would take his weight.

It was very bare on the other side—bare but safe—and there was room enough to lie down. Because of the rock projecting above the shallow cave, he would be in shadow most of the time. He could see a short stretch of the road above without being seen himself, and he could see the whole coastline toward the east.

David took his wet trousers off and spread them and his shirt out to dry in the sun. Then he unpacked his bundle and arranged his possessions neatly by his side—his compass, his knife, his bottle . . . the chunk of bread the man on board the ship had given him, and finally the round thing he had found. He held it firmly but carefully while he scratched it with his fingernail and bored his finger right through the skin. It was moist inside. He sniffed his finger and licked it—it smelled good and had a bittersweet taste. So he took the skin right off and pulled the inside apart. It was quite easy to separate into small pieces, each like a half moon. He was hungry, and he had a bit of bread as well. He wondered if that round thing were fit to eat.

Taking a bite, he chewed and swallowed and

waited to see what would happen. But nothing happened, nothing except that it tasted good. It did not make him ill.

David ate half the pieces and chewed a bit more bread. Then he tried the orange-colored peel, but that tasted sharp and unpleasant. He tried to push the thought away, but it kept returning: I don't *know* anything! How can I stay free when I don't know what everybody else knows! I don't even know what's good to eat and what's poisonous . . . the only food I know about is porridge and bread and soup . . .

For the moment he lost courage and felt quite cast down. Why had he not talked to the others in the camp, listened to their conversation and asked about the world outside? Not about food, of course, for there was a rule in the camp that no one might talk about food; for once, it was not one of *their* rules but one made by the prisoners themselves. When you had nothing but bread and porridge, and not enough of those, you did not want to talk about the kind of food you used to have when you were free. But there were other things he could have asked about. As long as Johannes had been with him, he had asked questions all the time, but he was only a little boy then and had asked about all sorts of things he had no use for now.

He looked out over the blue sea and down along

the coast full of bright color and sunshine and clenched his teeth. He would! It was no use sitting there thinking of all the things he ought to have done differently when he was in the camp; that could not be altered now.

He must think about Johannes and try to recall all they had talked about. He must remember, too, what he had heard the other prisoners say before they had been too long in the camp to say anything more and merely let the days drag by.

Sometimes he had discovered that they were trying to escape: they laid their plans, carefully weighing the pros and cons, calculating what they thought was possible, and making sure they knew where the worst dangers lay. Their attempts at escape were never successful, but that was not their fault: it was because their chances were too slender.

David decided to follow their example. He would make a plan of action, weighing what he knew against what he did not, and carry it out without allowing himself to be depressed by doubts or carried away by hope.

On his side was the fact that, although he was very thin, he had strong, tough muscles. He had sharp eyes and ears, and he was used to doing with very little food.

He stopped. Was there anything else to his credit?

Yes, he was prepared for *them*; he knew their methods, the traps they set, the sudden crafty friendliness that meant they were hiding something, their pointless brutality. He was familiar with treachery, and he knew what death looked like.

But what advantage was his knowledge of death when he was now determined to live? David frowned. Then he thought of another point in his favor: he could understand what people from different countries were talking about. Learning to do that had been a great help to him in the camp. When he could no longer pass the time thinking of mealtimes and the changing of the guard, there were various languages he could learn. David counted up how many he knew. First of course what *they* spoke— he could read that, too. Then he knew French . . . that was what Johannes had spoken. And besides that, German and Italian and English. He knew some Spanish and quite a bit of Hebrew.

Being able to talk to the sailor who had found him on board the ship had been a great advantage . . . and now that he was in Italy, his knowledge of the language would be a blessing to him. David felt greatly encouraged—perhaps he would recall other things he knew as he gradually grew accustomed to thinking again.

However, there were plenty of things he knew

nothing of. He knew there were maps, but he had never seen one, and he was quite ignorant of where the various countries of Europe lay or where their boundaries ran. He was not at all sure which of those countries were free; he thought there could not be many, and he had better reckon with the possibility that *they* were everywhere . . . even in free countries.

Then there was the business of food—he would have to live on what he could find, and every time he would have to risk eating something poisonous in his ignorance or passing by what was edible and so going hungry.

Worst of all, there were people. If he wanted to preserve his freedom, he would have to keep right away from them. But at the same time he realized he would have to get to know something about how people lived outside a prison camp, since an unknown danger was more dangerous than one that could be reckoned with beforehand.

And so David made another decision. When it was dark, he must go into the town that lay farther along the coast down by the sea. In the darkness he could always slip into a gateway or around a streetcorner as he had discovered in Salonika; but he would have to go while there were people about the streets so that he could find out how they lived.

Perhaps a boy among a crowd of people would appear less suspicious than a boy quite alone in a town where everyone was asleep.

In any case, it would not be as dangerous now as it might be later, for no one could yet know where to look for him. Perhaps they would not look for him at all?

Here again David ran into the blank wall of his own ignorance. He did not know who he was, did not even know from what country he had come. He had always lived in the camp, and even Johannes, who knew so many things, had not been able to find out anything about him for the simple reason that no one knew anything.

David wondered what he looked like. In the man's hut there had been a mirror, but it was hung too high. David had thought at one time that perhaps he was Jewish . . . As a rule, the people *they* imprisoned were those who wanted to decide for themselves what they should believe and be free to write books and articles about it. But that could not apply to him. Jews, on the other hand, were sometimes imprisoned just because *they* did not like Jews . . . They said they did, but it was not true.

But Johannes had said he was sure David was not Jewish.

Obviously one could not always find out why

they had arrested people, and if someone had happened to find him somewhere and taken him along to the camp when he was quite small, then it might be that he was not of sufficient consequence for them to make any particular effort to recapture him. But he could not be sure of that . . . and so it would be safer to assume that it was important for them to find him again.

David realized that he must have a story. He knew from his experiences in the camp that it might be a matter of life and death to "have a good story" and stick to it, however much one might be questioned. In the evening, when he had seen the kind of life people lived, he might perhaps be able to hit upon a story he could make use of if anyone questioned him. Not that he intended that anyone should speak to him if he could avoid it, but it was best to be prepared.

No one took any notice of him. While he was on the road, a man had turned around to look at him, but David had told himself, "You mustn't look as if you're afraid! You mustn't look afraid . . ." and had gone on his way quite calmly. And down here in the town no one at all turned to look at him. It was a small town, not like Salonika. The streets were small and narrow and very hilly. There was talk everywhere—people walking along with baskets and parcels, people standing in shops where the lights were lit, all were talking. The first time David was aware of it he could hardly bring himself to move on—almost everybody was laughing! It was not the ugly laughter he was used to when *they* laughed at the prisoners—it sounded pleasant, even beautiful, as if they were all content with life and felt friendly toward one another.

David knew, of course, that his impression could not be right, but perhaps there were not so many of *them* here in Italy, or perhaps there just were not any in this town. And the people were beautiful! David had seen good-looking people before—they were often good looking when they first arrived in the camp, but only Johannes had preserved a beauty of expression right up to the time of his death. And the few women David had seen looked quite different from those here. They had been hard of face, as *they* always were, and . . . and . . . yes, as if there were scarcely any difference between them and the men.

But here they were beautiful, their hair long, black, and waving, many of them with smooth sun-tanned faces, and all dressed in beautiful clothes of many colors, like the sea and the trees and the golden fruit.

David saw the same fruit again, a whole pile of it in a great basket outside a shop. *"Arancia,"* it was called. David suddenly recalled a German word. *"Apfelsinen"*—he had heard of it after all. If only the letters were not so difficult to read! Johannes had taught him the shapes of the letters they used in other countries, but that was so long ago. If only he had a book so that he could practice reading those letters!

Going down into the town had been a good move. No one took any notice of him, and he could learn a lot by looking in the shops. He could find out what food looked like, and many other things, too, that he had never seen before and did not know the use of. They had an enormous number of possessions, these people.

David felt quite dizzy with looking at so many things, and he stopped a moment. In front of him a man and a woman were walking along, and as they talked and laughed together, they were eating something they had bought from a shop. When they finished, the woman threw away the newspaper that had been wrapped around what they had been eating. His heart beating faster, David picked it up in the dark; there was often something printed on the paper things were wrapped in.

He hurried on to the nearest light—yes, there

was printing on it, something he could practice read-ing! Tomorrow when it grew light . . . He dared not stand still too long outside a brightly lit shop; be-sides, he did not feel too well. He had a headache and felt sick. He had better go back to his rock now.

He looked up and discovered he was standing in a large square. At first he was frightened, for he felt much safer in the narrow streets, but then he forgot his fear as he saw in front of him on the other side of the square a very big building with what he took to be a searchlight on top.

A prison camp? For a moment David's heart stopped beating, so panic-stricken was he. Then he noticed a large bell hanging in a tower. A church! "If there's a bell, then it's a church," he remembered Johannes had once told him. But he did not tell him that a church could be so beautiful . . . its walls built of different kinds of stone that formed intricate and lovely patterns, its great doors approached by a magnificent flight of steps. David looked at the church for a long time. He felt it had some meaning for him, but he could not tell what. His head felt very heavy as if he had been running all night long; he must return to his hideout.

Slowly he turned his back upon the square and went down into the narrow, brightly lit streets again.

He stopped outside a shop where they baked round flat loaves with what he had learned were called tomatoes on top. He was hungry. Not very hungry at the moment, but he would be by the morning. He had once seen a guard shoot a prisoner for trying to steal his food. Perhaps in the morning he would find another orange.

He turned to go.

"Hi, want one, eh?"

David turned around with a start. The man was standing in the open doorway offering him one of the loaves. David automatically put out his hand—and then he quickly withdrew it. A trap. He would take the bread and then the man would fetch *them* . . .

He looked up into the man's face and saw it was just like the sailor's . . . the same slightly stupid expression, the same good-natured eyes. David hesitated . . . Perhaps he would not have him arrested. There were *some* good people—Johannes had told him so—and he had heard the same thing from other prisoners; they had often spoken of those who had helped them and hidden them for long periods when *they* were after them.

The man laughed in a hearty, friendly way, the way everybody laughed here. "Well! Perhaps the young fellow isn't hungry!" he said.

"Yes. Yes, I am," David answered. "Thank you

very much!" He took the bread, and off he went with quick, unhurried steps. The man frowned and looked at him a little puzzled. Then he shrugged his shoulders right up to his ears and let them fall again, as if he were shaking something off, and went back to his loaves.

Never in the whole of David's life had a day passed so quickly as did the next one. Still free, he had gotten back to his rocks again, eaten half the bread the man had given him, and lain down to sleep. When he awoke, it was day, and everything was just as warm and beautiful in the bright sunshine as it had been on the previous day. He had run up to the little stream to wash before anyone was about, and even the fact that his soap had grown much thinner from overmuch use the day before did not really trouble him. Perhaps it was because he had washed his shirt and trousers with it as well—he decided to make do with washing his hands and feet and face that day and to go sparingly with his precious soap. Then he ran downhill again, nearly forgetting, in his eagerness to get back to his piece of paper, to look carefully up and down the road before he crossed it. That must not happen again! He made himself count to a hundred before he picked up his paper in order to remind himself how important it was never to do anything without thinking.

The scrap of newspaper was difficult to read. The evening before he had read several notices in the town, but this was in proper sentences with many words together. David murmured the names of the letters to himself, first one by one and then running them together three or four at a time, and after a bit the sounds began to take shape as words he already knew. Then he began reading to himself what was on the paper. On the whole it proved disappointing; some of it was about things you could buy, but none of it was any use to a boy escaping from prison. There was something about motorcars, and the last bit was about a king. But at that point the paper was torn across, and David could not even find out where the king came from.

From what he had heard in the camp, David had gathered that the countries that had kings were free, and their people had no need to be frightened of *them*.

But there were not many countries like that, and the knowledge was not of much use to him since he did not know where those countries were.

However, his belief that he might perhaps avoid capture seemed to have grown stronger since the day before. He had seen so much in the town that he knew deep within himself he would have to go down there again, but he would not yet admit it to himself. He was pulled both ways: he had a passionate desire to go back and learn more about what things were like outside the camp, and at the same time he was afraid he might forget to hide his fears.

As long as it was still daylight, he would think no more about paying another visit to the town. He had plenty of other things to occupy him: all that he had seen the previous day, all that he wanted to know and would have to find out for himself. And there was his piece of paper; even if it contained nothing of any use to him, he could always read the letters, comparing the words as they appeared in print with the way they sounded when they were spoken until he was sure he could read properly. And in between times, when his head began to buzz with the weight of too many problems that seemed to have no solution, there were his beautiful surroundings that he would never tire of looking at. The blue sea stretching farther than eye could reach and the land with its ever-changing coastline . . . the green hills, the bare red rocks . . . the brightly colored houses gleaming like fruit here and there in the sun.

When evening came, David went down to the town again. And again the next evening, and the next . . . and each time he learned something new, enough to occupy his thoughts all day long in his rocky hiding place. And although he knew there must be many things he had no idea of, this was not brought home to him until the third evening when he saw a little baby.

A woman was sitting on her doorstep. There was not much light, and so David slackened his pace when he saw something moving in her lap. It was very tiny and it was alive, but it was not an animal. It slowly dawned upon him that it must be a very young baby. David was fascinated; he could not drag himself away, and yet he dared not stay there. Then the woman laughed, quite softly, as if one should not laugh out loud in the presence of so small a child, and she said to him, "Do you like him? Don't you think he's a beautiful boy?"

Hesitantly David took a step forward as he looked up and down the street . . . but there was no one to notice that the woman had spoken to him. He stepped right up to her and bent his head down to see better. The woman lifted the baby up as if she wanted it to stand in her lap, but it could not. The child was such a tiny little thing that it could not even support itself on its own two legs! Such tiny hands, smaller than the box he kept his matches in . . . but its eyes were big and black, with long thick lashes, and they looked straight into his face as if they were quite ignorant of fear.

David's own eyes smarted as if he wanted to cry. What did you do with a child as small as that? A child that could not even run, that did not even know you had to be afraid . . . What dreadful things could happen to a little child like that!

For the first time David spoke to someone of his own accord. He had to. She could know nothing about it, this woman who was able to laugh. He looked into her smiling face and said, trembling with anxiety, "Oh, you *must* look after him! You mustn't forget him for a single moment! He's so terribly small that he can do nothing for himself, and one blow might crush him . . . You must take care all the time, or else he'll never grow big enough to look after himself . . ."

He stopped, frightened. The woman was not smiling anymore—she looked as if she were afraid herself now. Then she recovered and, smiling again, said he could depend upon it, she would take good care of the child. She spoke as if she would comfort him, and yet it was not he who stood in need of comfort—it was that poor little child that could not protect itself.

David could not bear to stay in the town any longer that evening. He ran all the way back to his rocks, and even when at last he fell asleep, he found no relief, for he dreamed all night long of the terrible things that could happen to such a tiny baby, and during his dreams he kept half waking up with the feeling that he was too stupid and knew too little to do anything about it. For the first time in his life David knew that he could feel fear for others.

But when at last he was fully awake, the sun was shining just as it had done the day before.

His first thought was to wonder if the baby was still safe. He ought not to have left it: the woman clearly had no idea how dangerous it was for a child to be so small—and he, David, who knew the danger, had left it unprotected!

It was David's first encounter with his conscience. What was the right thing to do? He had not really any doubt: he realized vaguely that one was always quite sure what the right thing was. And it was most important to do what one knew was right, for otherwise the day might come when one could no longer tell the difference between right and wrong, and then one would be like *them*.

David slowly got ready to go back into the town to find the baby and look after it. He now wanted to go on living—there was such a mass of things he wanted to know before *they* caught him again—but not if it meant being like *them*.

He had already laid the plank in position when he seemed to hear a voice say, "Think what you're doing! Remember what you promised yourself—you were never going to do anything without thinking carefully first!"

David sat down again. There could be no doubt about it: the right thing was to look after the child . . . David frowned. But *could* he? Would he who knew so much less about life than anyone else be any good at it? Someone had to look after the child, but he was not necessarily the one to do it . . . Perhaps, after all, the young woman could do it better—now that he had warned her how important it was.

Perhaps she was the baby's mother? Most people had mothers, and mothers always cared for their children, even when the children were grown up.

With a sense of relief, David pulled the plank back again and told himself he had been a fool . . . That was what happened when you did not stop to think. In the camp, thinking would have made life unbearable, but when you were free, it was necessary, though something of a strain when you were not used to it. The most important thing of all, he felt quite sure, was to do what you knew to be right. But, at the same time, you must not forget to think carefully before you acted. Just suppose he had made a mistake with the baby because he did not know what it needed!

David decided he would think about it as little

as possible. It still pained him to remember how small and helpless the baby was, but since he could not look after it properly, it would be best to forget about it.

But how was it that he had not seen a baby before? There must have been babies about on the other evenings he had spent in the the town. The thought worried him; there might have been other things he had passed by without noticing . . . Johannes had once said he was very intelligent. He had not meant David to hear him, and he had looked very sad as he spoke—but that was probably because it was best not to think about anything in the camp.

But if he were intelligent, how was it things could happen under his nose without his being aware of them? Perhaps because he was trying to learn too much at once; and yet he knew he had to . . .

David had hit upon a good story. During his second evening he had read something on a wall about a circus. He understood it was a kind of theater that traveled about; if anyone questioned him, he would say he came from one and was going to rejoin it somewhere else—somewhere far enough away to prevent people finding out immediately if it were true.

But he had had no occasion to try his story out.

He went down to the town again during the evening. He was gradually getting to know it inside out—the narrow crooked streets, the open space down by the seafront, the square where the church stood. He always went there last of all so that on the way back to the rock he would have fresh in mind the beautiful wall with its patterns of variegated stone. He had not summoned up enough courage to enter the church, although he would have dearly loved to see what it looked like inside.

That evening he took care to avoid the street where the woman sat with her baby. He was sure now that she must know better than he how to look after it, but he would rather not be reminded that the child was too young to understand the dangers that beset it.

There were plenty of other streets. David would sometimes stand in the shadows outside a shop and listen to the conversation within. It was easy enough, for they always talked very loudly, with frequent bursts of laughter. In that way he learned what many things were used for, things that were strange to him but seemed to be taken for granted by the people around him.

He had not yet heard anyone talk about *them*; sometimes the fact that there were obviously none of them in the town led him to be rather less careful.

He always walked on if anyone looked at him, but he sometimes came very near to forgetting his fears, and he quite openly filled his bottle at the pump down by the seafront and accepted several loaves of bread from the man who made them. At first he would stand for a long time hidden in the shadows outside the shop, listening to the baker's conversation with his customers—but it was never about *them*, and he never asked David any questions except whether he was hungry, and then he would give him a loaf and a friendly smile.

And so it was almost out of habit that David now hid in the dark outside and listened. That evening the man was talking of someone called Guglio and the good catch he had had. For a moment David's heart stood still with fear . . . Then he realized they were talking, not of people, but of fish caught at sea.

He stood there a little longer, forgetting in his relief to listen. Suddenly he heard the man say, "Who's that boy that comes here every evening for a loaf? Do you know?"

"What boy?"

"A thin, ragged boy, but always very clean . . . He looks a bit foreign . . ."

David pressed himself flat against the wall and stood there as if glued to the spot. Another man was speaking now, one who spoke differently from the rest, more after David's own fashion. "I've seen a strange boy every evening this week; he stands and looks at the church. I assumed he'd come over for the harvest. Signor Missiani takes on a number of casual workers about this time . . ."

Then a woman said something. "No one's come yet, Padre. Therese would have told me . . . I've seen the boy, too. It must be the same one. He doesn't look like the others, and he always moves off when you look at him. He's got very strange-looking eyes . . ."

"In what way strange?" That was the one they called Padre speaking again. "Padre" meant "priest." "I've only seen him standing in the dark on the other side of the square . . . Does he look as if he's on the downward path?"

"No, no . . . I don't know about that, Padre, but he's a strange boy . . . If you smile at him, he doesn't smile back. He doesn't run off, either; he just turns and walks away. And his eyes . . . they're so quiet-looking. Perhaps we should get hold of him and ask him where he comes from . . ."

David heard no more. With no more sound than a puff of wind, he was down the street and inside the first open door—through a long dark passage and out again in another street. Never before had he found it so difficult to walk along calmly, as if he felt no fear. He increased his speed . . . out of the town, out to the rocks—he must get away at once before they began looking for him.

They might be sending for *them* already . . . David waited a long time, a very long time, hiding by the side of the road, before he ventured scrambling down to his hiding place. The last two evenings he had left his bundle there, and now he must take it with him. But first he had to make sure no one was following.

When he reached the safety of the rocks, he lay down, but not to sleep, only because his legs felt as if they would not bear his weight any longer. As he lay there, he could see the lights from the town below. They looked beautiful in the dark. But he had been right when he sensed there was danger there; he must get away this very night.

The thought filled him with gloom. He had begun to feel that it was his town, that the rock belonged to him. He knew every little irregularity in its surface, and every morning when he undid his bundle, he would arrange his things in the same way. The little stream higher up across the road had been his alone, and every morning he had found an orange.

All the beauty of the place had been his: the sea and the coastline that curved along its shores; all the beautiful colors, the blues and greens and reds; and the gay houses, brightly colored, too, and gleaming like fruit in the sunlight.

Before he had come to this place, he had known about nothing but death; there he had learned to live, to be the master of his own fate; he had learned what it felt like to wash in clean water in the sunshine until he was clean himself, and what it felt like to satisfy his hunger with food that tasted good; he had learned the sound of laughter that was free from cruelty; he had learned the meaning of beauty—and now he must leave it and never return.

David cried—but not for long. He sat up and looked once more at the lights of the town. He had also learned to think again without being afraid of doing it.

And he could go on thinking; he was now his own master, and if he thought about everything carefully, as clearly and sensibly as he could, and remembered all he had learned in this place, then freedom might be his for a long time yet.

He had been right in supposing that *they* were everywhere, even where he was now. But he had also found it true that some people were good and kind. The woman had not informed against him, nor had the man who had given him bread. And if they no longer dared to pretend that they had not seen him about, then it was his own fault for staying there too long. In the future he must never stay in one place longer than one evening. He must continue to avoid people as much as possible, and he must remember not to look at them.

David wished he knew what was so strange about his eyes. What did they mean when they said they were quiet? Perhaps one day he might come across a mirror and find out what he looked like. David sighed a little: he might find it difficult to remember about his eyes all the time. But a boy could not very well disguise himself. Grown men could grow beards or shave them off; and if you had money, you could change your clothes, or wear glasses, or dye your hair. But when you were a boy with neither beard nor money, it was no good thinking about disguising yourself. It would not help very much, anyway, if it were your eyes that people recognized.

David packed everything except his compass into his bundle and stood up. When he had crossed over the plank, he drew it after him and carried it right up to the roadway so that no one would see where he had been living. He stood still for a moment and looked down at the lights of the town. If the people down there had been really good, like those who risked everything to hide others from *them*, they would have let him stay.

David turned his back on the lights and set off quietly up the mountain slope toward the north.

3

Tired out and scratched to pieces, David was glad when it began to grow light. He was no longer used to traveling at night and decided that, as soon as he had gotten far enough away, he would travel during the day instead. Traveling by night was too exhausting in a terrain where at every step you might run into something or trip over it—plants, tree roots, an unexpected rise or a hole in the ground. He had noticed, too, that as long as people were not able to take a good look at him, they paid him little enough attention—he was just a boy passing by. There must be many boys like himself. The many things he must have failed to notice in the town continued to fret him. There might have been boys there, too, but he had been so busy learning about what was in the shops, listening to what people talked about and reading notices, that he had not been aware of them. He could read anything now, as long as it was in print, and that was a great advantage.

He waited till it was light enough to see whether there were houses nearby and then found a good clump of bushes to sleep in.

But when he awoke, he had a shock. He awoke while it was still daylight, and as he sat up, he found himself looking straight out to sea! He looked anxiously at his compass and then at the sea again. Perhaps the compass had broken? He turned around with it in his hand, but the needle moved as it should. Some way off he could hear the sound of cars, and he was still high above sea level. For a moment he thought he had lost his way in the dark and had wandered in a circle till he was back again in the neighborhood of the town. Then another thought occurred to him: perhaps the coastline curved right around and he had crossed a strip of land with the sea on both sides of it. Yes, that was it! David rose quickly to his feet and made his way down toward the shore until he could see along the coast. He found he had been right. The point where land and sea and sky faded into one another, blurred into the same shade of blue, now lay in the opposite direction—on his right as he stood facing the sea, instead of on his left as it had done from his rock.

But what now? He must go northward: that was

what the man had told him. For the first time since he had arrived in Italy, David could think about the man calmly and dispassionately. He had told him to go north till he came to a country called Denmark. But why should he do what the man told him? Was not he David, his own master, who decided for himself? In the camp, of course, you had to obey the man. He was the commandant, and it had never occurred to David not to obey him. He had seen only too often what happened if you failed to obey even an ordinary guard.

But now there was no longer any reason to obey him. Or was there? The bundle *had* lain under the tree, and when he had gone south, he *had* come to Salonika. And there *had* been a ship sailing for Italy there. He had not yet discovered any trap set for him by the man—but perhaps there was one in that country called Denmark. It was all very puzzling, and David could find no answer. How could he put any trust in what the man had told him to do when he knew more surely than anything else in the world that the man hated him and always had?

"But I've no need to worry about that now," he said to himself. "If the bit of Italy I've been in so far juts out into the sea as I think it does, then I'd better go more to the east, for that's the direction the land seems to follow. And if I stay free long enough, I may even find out why the man hated me and was still prepared to let me go."

On this side of the peninsula, too, the road wound along on a kind of shelf above the sea. David crossed it, keeping his eyes fixed on the ground—he might find an orange, and he had not much bread left. He did find one—he found a tree covered with them! He had not realized that oranges grew on trees. There was not much traffic on the road, only an occasional car passing by, and the lowest branches of the tree were within reach and easy to climb. David picked two oranges—it would be a good thing to have one in reserve. Then he found a comfortable place to sit on a flat rock and settled down to his breakfast. A little bit of bread, water—fresh and clear, not muddy and tasteless like the water in the camp—and then an orange to finish with.

But he had better be on his way; if *they* had begun to search for him, he must get away quickly. They had no photographs they could recognize him by—that was a point in his favor. He stood up, and as he stumbled over a loose stone, his compass went flying over the edge of the rock where he had been sitting, farther and farther down at such a rate that before he could put his hand out, it was too late.

All he could do was to follow it with his eyes

until it disappeared into the sea so far below that he could not even hear the plop.

The sea was very deep under the rocks, and David knew he would never find the compass again. He sat for a long time staring at the place where it had disappeared. He was lost now. Now he *would* go around in circles and keep coming back to the same place. And *they* would find him.

He had had so little. Now he had nothing, nothing at all to safeguard his freedom.

"God!" he said softly. "Oh, God!"

He did not know why . . . it was what the men sometimes said in the camp when they were most in despair. But as for himself, he had no God.

And no compass either. Freedom was precious, and he had nothing to ensure it.

Then David decided that he must have a God: it might possibly help. But which God should he choose? It was important to find the right one. If only he had listened more carefully to what the men had talked about in the camp! He had been so interested in learning new words that he had often missed the point of the conversation. If he had asked more questions, he would have learned a lot more.

What gods did he know of? The one the Jews had made so many sacrifices for in return for His help. What had David to give? Nothing! And if you were not a Jew, perhaps you had no right to choose Him. And the God of the Catholics seemed to leave things to a woman called Mary. Not that David had anything against women, but he knew so little about them that it would probably be better to choose one who looked after things Himself. Johannes should have taught him something about God. Instead, he had only told him about a man, also called David, who had lived a long time ago. David dug into his memory; when he thought hard, he could recall many of the things Johannes had said. Was not there something about a God, too, in that story about David? Something in rather difficult words—he had always liked new words that were long and strange: he enjoyed finding out what they meant.

Suddenly it came back to him. That other David had said of his God, "He maketh me to lie down in green pastures: He leadeth me beside the still waters."

He was the one he would choose!

Clutching his orange tightly, he first looked around to make sure there was no one who could overhear him, and then he said in a low voice, "God of the green pastures and the still waters, I am David and I choose You as my God! But You must please understand that I can't do anything for You, because I've always been in a wicked place where no one could think or learn or get to know anything, and so I know nothing about what people ought to do for their God. But the David Johannes used to talk about knew that even if he couldn't see You, You were there and were stronger than any men. I pray You will help me so that *they* won't catch me again. Then perhaps I can gradually find out about You so that I can do something in return. And if You know where Johannes is now, will You please thank him for me for going with me to Salonika and tell him, now that I'm free, I can think about him again. I am David. Amen."

Perhaps it was a mistake to say "amen" because that was what Catholics did, but David knew it was a holy word, and if you did not have an ending, God would not know when you had finished your prayer.

He felt a sense of relief and added strength just as he had the morning he had determined to go on living. He was glad he had thought of it: a God would be a lot better than a compass . . . though, of course, it would have been nice to have both.

During the course of the evening he had almost reached the point where the coastline bore to the left, and from the position of the sun he could see that if he continued in the same direction, he would be going roughly northwest. Every evening, and every morning, too, when he woke up, he would be able to tell by the sun which way he was going; he would manage even if he had lost his compass.

It had been a good day . . . everywhere it had been beautiful, and in a little town he had found one of those water faucets that people drank from. Perhaps there was one in every town. And he had not met *them* anywhere. There had not been any cars of the sort *they* rode in either, and David once again felt sure that he would pull through and might remain free for a long time yet.

Bread was his chief problem. There was so much to eat in Italy that people would leave food lying about without realizing it—an orange or a tomato—but never bread, and bread you had to have if you were not to starve.

David sat down by the roadside. People often did that, and so he felt free to do so, too. After a while he took the precaution of lying flat on his stomach and facing the road, and he made sure he could quickly duck out of sight if anything came along. He lay thinking about various things. During the course of that day he had discovered that unless a town were very small, its name appeared on a notice some distance ahead, and if there were only one figure after the name, then the town was not very far off. The figure, he thought, perhaps meant how many kilometers you had to go. He thought, too, that if he did not find any bread the next day, he would have to ask God for some. Meanwhile, dusk was falling rapidly, and a car suddenly pulled up within a few yards of where he lay.

David ducked. A man got out of the car and began rummaging in the trunk. David raised his head—he was quite an ordinary man, not one of *them*. The man made a sudden movement, and David heard him mutter, "Blast, my glasses!"

He spoke in English, not Italian. As he watched the man groping about in the half light along the edge of the road, David rose to his feet. When people wore glasses, they could not see anything without them . . . "I'll help you find your glasses . . ."

The man straightened, bent toward him, and peered into his face. David cast his eyes down, drew back slightly, and wished he had thought first. But the man smiled and said, "Thank you very much! It's not much good looking for glasses when you haven't got them on, is it?"

David answered, "No," politely, and set about searching the edge of the road carefully until he came across them. The man had stepped over to the car and was talking to someone inside as David stood by with the glasses in his hand . . . Was he one of *them* after all? Could he escape? How far could he get? It was only a second before the stranger turned around and said, "Can't you find them? If you can't, my wife will drive . . ."

David stepped slowly forward. "Here they are," he said, and added hesitantly, "sir." The man put the glasses on and smiled again, and David felt sure he was not one of *them*. He had quite a different look about him; David could not imagine him striking or shooting anyone. He now felt in his pocket, took something out, and offered it to David. A coin lay in his hand. "You must have something for your trouble," he said.

"No," said David quickly, stepping back. "I mean—no, thank you."

The stranger looked a little disconcerted; then he smiled and said in that case David must accept his thanks and asked if he would like to say, "How do you do?" to his wife.

David did not really want to, but as he did not know how to say so, he went with him to the car. A woman sat inside. She was not beautiful like the women of Italy, but she had a pleasant clean smell, and it was not yet too dark for him to see that she was smiling. So David said good evening to her.

Then the man spoke to her in French; he asked her if she had ever before come across a little Italian tramp who spoke English with an Oxford accent and was offended when he was offered money.

David was just about to say that he had not been offended when he decided not to. Since they already thought it strange that he spoke English, it was better not to let them see that he understood French as well.

They asked him what he was called and who he was. David replied that his name was David and he was on his way to join a circus farther north. Fortunately, they did not seem very interested, and apparently taking a hint from the brevity of his answer, they questioned him no more. Instead they told him they came from England, were on a holiday, and would shortly have to return. Then the woman suggested they should have something she called "sandwiches." These turned out to be food—slices of bread with something between them. They asked David if he would like one, and he said, "Yes, please."

They seemed pleased when David accepted their offer, and David thought they might be willing to answer a question if he put one to them.

"Is there a king in England?" he inquired.

The man told him that at the moment there was a queen because the last king had had no sons, only daughters. She was a good queen, he said, and beautiful, too, and she had a very fine golden crown.

David looked at him in surprise. What did it

matter what she had? All that really mattered was that the people of England would be free, as people always were in those countries that had kings—or, of course, queens.

He ate the last mouthful. "I've finished, sir . . . Can I go now?"

The woman leaned over toward him. "Yes, of course you can . . . but . . . David, I would like to see you smile."

David felt awkward; her face had an anxious look, as if she were waiting for him to give her something. But he had nothing to give. "I . . . I'm sorry; I don't know how to do it . . ." He turned away slightly and asked again, "Can I go now, sir?"

In a low voice the woman said rapidly in French, "Donald, we can't let him go like that . . . He's about the same age as our own boys . . . He might be English. You can see he's not an ordinary little tramp . . . Those eyes . . . can't you see his eyes?"

The man laid his hand on hers and broke in. "Yes, I can, and the boy's frightened; the longer you keep him here, the more frightened he grows. We can't get mixed up in it, Alice, and I'm sure he's not English . . ."

Then to David, "You're not English, David, are you?"

Almost before he had finished speaking, David

answered quickly, "No, sir . . . There was a man in the . . . in the circus who was English . . ." He had very nearly said "in the camp" but had corrected himself in time. "Won't you let me go? I didn't take your food before you said I could . . ."

"Of course you may go, David." The man's voice sounded almost like Johannes'. "If there were any way in which we could help you, you would tell us, wouldn't you?"

"Yes, sir. There isn't. Thank you. Good-bye." He was in such a hurry to get away, he stumbled over his words. Then off he ran before they could stop him again. He ran back along the road, and before he reached the first bend, he lay down in the ditch and looked back at the car. It stayed there a long time before it drove off.

It was growing quite dark now.

David began to clamber slowly down the slope toward the sea to find himself a place to sleep for the night. He was thinking about the strangers . . . English people from a free country. They were obviously kind . . . and yet they did not seem willing to let him go, especially the woman. She seemed to think she ought to keep him there. David could not understand it . . . but when he searched his mind for what he knew about countries that were free, he found the answer: in those countries they had a kind

of police force to help those who had not done anything wrong. She was only there on a holiday, and
perhaps she had no idea how different things were
in other countries. The thought was comforting. He
had been alarmed at the idea that she would delib-
erately set out to ensnare him—there would be a
sort of treachery in giving him food and smiling at
him and then seeking to hold on to him. But if she
were ignorant of the situation, then there was nothing sinister in what she had done. Only he must
take more care and remember not to look at people
long enough for them to notice his eyes. It would
be helpful if he could find a mirror—if he knew
what was wrong with his eyes, he might be able to
do something about it. And he would have to learn
to smile. People had sometimes smiled at him in
the town, and then they had looked put out, as if
they regretted having done it. If you could smile
back every time people smiled at you, perhaps they
would take less notice of you.

David was just on the point of falling asleep
when what seemed a very important idea struck him.
The Englishman had wanted to give him money! He
had refused it, to be sure, but only because he had
had such a . . . such a strong impulse to do something quite voluntarily for another person . . . not
to be ordered to do it, but to do it without anyone's

saying he had to, without anyone's being ready to take it out on him if he did not. It had felt almost like possessing something, something so big that he could give some of it away. If he had taken the money, it would not have felt the same. But in the future he might perhaps be able to find things to do that he could get money for; then he could buy bread every day. He would not be able to avoid people, of course, but if only he could get to the bottom of what was wrong with his eyes and learn how to smile, then perhaps he would manage after all.

And manage he did during the following weeks. Only two days later, in a town called Naples, he found a small mirror. A woman walking along the street dropped it. A corner broke off, and so she made a face and left it there. David waited till she was out of sight and then picked it up; you could still see yourself in it, anyway. Clutching it in his hand, he walked on till he came to a place where there were trees and dried grass right in the middle of the town. There was a seat, and there David sat down and held up the mirror.

At first his hand shook so much he could not see properly, but very soon a face appeared clearly in the mirror—his own!

It did not look ugly. No, he honestly could not

see what could be wrong with it. It was thin, but so were many people's faces. The color of his hair perhaps was not quite right; possibly it should have been a darker brown. He held the mirror close to his face to take a good look at his eyes. Johannes had had blue eyes. Here in Italy they all had dark brown or black eyes. But you could have other colors. David strove to recall what the eyes of the men in the camp had looked like, but all he could remember clearly was that they were dull, whereas his own now looked very bright. Was there something wrong with dark gray eyes? Perhaps there was a touch of green in them if you looked carefully. He still could not understand in what way they were strange, and so he dismissed the thought—there was nothing else to do but look away when anyone looked at him for any length of time.

Many times a day during the days that followed he took out his mirror and practiced smiling, but he could not get it right, he could not make it look the way it did when other people smiled, and in the end he gave it up.

He continued to go northward. Not that he wanted to do as the man had told him, but he obviously had to go somewhere, and that was the direction the English people had taken. Without being fully aware of it, David had some idea at the back of his mind that he might perhaps go to England . . .

During his first days of freedom he had had but one thought from morning to night: when he woke up, it had taken the form, "If *they* haven't caught me by this evening . . ." and as he lay down to sleep, "If *they* don't catch me tomorrow . . ." He now began to believe that he might possibly remain free for a long time to come—perhaps until winter overtook him. And as soon as he opened his eyes in the morning to the pleasant warmth of the sun, he would feel sure that he would reach a country where he could live in safety.

The idea of earning some money had been a good one. He had earned no money in Naples, but he had fetched coffee for people who sat eating in a restaurant and the waiter had given him a loaf of bread for his pains. And in a small town farther north he had been given money by some strangers who were afraid of having their luggage stolen from the car while they went into the church. He had heard them talking and had offered to stand by and keep an eye on their things until they came back. He realized afterward that he did not know what he would have done if anyone had attempted to take the bags, but fortunately nobody had tried, and he had been given so much money that he was able to buy enough bread for two days.

David's chief difficulty was that people asked so many questions, but as he gained in experience from all he saw about him, he was gradually able to improve upon his story of the circus. He had learned by this time that people had no evil intentions when they questioned him, and since he was pretty good at slipping away before they began to look too anxiously at him, he was no longer quite so frightened. The Italians did not ask so many questions, but it was easier to earn money from the tourists who were on vacation from other countries, and so David embroidered his tale of the circus until he thought it sounded absolutely genuine. When he was asked where he was going to rejoin the circus, he would invent a name so that however suspicious his questioners might be afterward, they would not be able to trace him.

The sun continued to shine with a pleasant warmth day by day, but it was now beginning to grow cold at night. David was quite determined, however, never to enter a house. Houses were dangerous places; you never knew but what someone might be standing in the doorway barring your exit the very moment you wanted to slip away.

Every time he came to a town, he would walk

around till he found the church. He promised himself that if he was not caught and came to a country where he could live in security, he would go inside one and see what it looked like. Not that he really expected that he would be able to preserve his freedom long enough for that; it was best not to be too sure. But sometimes when he had had enough to eat and found a comfortable place to sleep in and sat gazing at the hills and valleys and the sun shining on the distant mountains, he could not help feeling that perhaps he *might* be lucky.

It was now a long time since he had seen the sea, but although he missed it, there was plenty to interest him. There did not seem to be one dull, uninspiring place in the whole of Italy. All his life David had seen nothing but the same ugly, flat gray scene, and now he never grew tired of tramping through the ever-changing countryside. Every time he came to a bend in the road, he was afraid the beauty of the scene would disappear, but each time a new beauty was revealed in the constantly changing landscape of green and undulating hills and valleys. David had now learned what some of the trees were called. There were olives with their gnarled trunks and pale gray-green leaves, whispering and quivering in the lightest breeze as if they were alive, and there were cypresses, tall and slender, pointing straight up into the sky. Best of all were those places where a river flowed through the valley bottom. There he could sit for hours on end wondering where the river came from and where it ran to.

There, too, he could wash. His piece of soap had grown quite small now, although he did not use it every day; he dared not wash in the towns when he filled his water bottle at the pump, for he had never seen anyone washing there and it might have been forbidden.

It was Sunday today, the day the people were most full of laughter and the shops were shut. That did not matter since David had not earned any money for two days and could not have bought bread, anyway. He had found a bunch of grapes, however, and he was used to doing with very little food. It would soon be evening, and he was sitting by the roadside thinking over a plan he had had in mind since the day before. He could not make up his mind whether he dared try it. The day before he had seen a man walking along the road, and when a car came by, he had held up his hand and stopped it. The driver had put his head out and asked if the other wanted a lift, and the man who had been walking said yes, please, he did.

But you had to say where you were going—and suppose the driver became suspicious? In that case you were caught—you could not get out. David trembled at the thought but still could not quite give up the idea. A car traveled at an immense speed, and if he kept going in the same direction, he must at some point leave Italy behind. It was very beautiful there, but as the days went by, David seemed to prize his freedom more and more. When he had first arrived and was living on the rocks by the sea, his freedom had not meant so much to him, since he had not expected it to last more than a day or two. But now that he had enjoyed it so long, he could no longer think of giving it up.

As his fear of losing his freedom had grown, his desire to reach a place of safety had become so strong that he could now think of nothing else. David wondered whether it were always like that—whether when you had something, you not only wanted to keep it but wanted something else as well . . . It seemed greedy, but he could not help it. Freedom and a country where he could live in safety: David wanted both. "But nothing more," he told himself. "Just those two things and that will be enough. Johannes said greedy people can never be happy, and I would so much like to know what it feels like to be happy. Johannes said that when you very much want something you haven't got, you no longer care for what you have got. I'm not sure that I understand, but I suppose he meant that things are only worth having if you think they are."

David tried to forget that he also wanted a new piece of soap. If he could preserve his freedom and reach a free country, he must be satisfied with that. And if he could bring himself to ask for a lift, he would get to another country all the more quickly. If only he could find out whereabouts those other countries lay! He dared not ask anyone, for if you said you belonged to a circus, then you would be expected to know your way about, and so it might prove dangerous to show your ignorance.

David's thoughts were disturbed by the sound of a car. It sounded wrong, as though the engine were not running properly. He lay down flat in the grass and watched it crawl along at no more than a walking pace. It was American, not Italian; he had long since taught himself the meaning of the letters on license plates.

Americans were most likely good people, for they were the ones *they* hated most. All that was wrong with them, David thought, was that they spoke English very oddly and always acted as if they were proud of possessing so much.

There was one thing, however, that these two Americans did not possess: they had no gas, as they called petrol, and that was why their car would not go. David stood up and took a step toward them.

The woman was talking in a loud, angry voice that did not sound at all pleasant, and David was more nervous than he usually was when he was going to speak to someone. But she stopped when he asked the man if he could help by fetching some gas for them.

They were both very glad to accept his offer, and David suggested that he take their can and go to the village farther up the side of the hill. "But I haven't any money to pay for the gas," he said as he took the can.

The man was about to take some money out of his pocket when the woman said quickly, "He's nothing but a young beggar, Dick! You can be quite sure if we give him money, we shall never see him again! He can get help from a garage up there . . ."

She did not of course intend David to understand what she said. He wondered if they thought he was stupid; they seemed to think he could understand only when they spoke very slowly.

The man asked him if he could get a mechanic to drive down with the gas. "The can's a bit heavy for you to carry," he said.

David turned his back on the woman. "The people here don't like doing very much on Sundays, and so I can't be sure I can find anyone willing to drive down," he explained politely. "But I'll see if I can get the gas by promising to pay for it later. Unless, of course, your wife thinks I want to keep your can."

The man looked uncomfortable.

"That wouldn't work, boy," he said. "Then you'd have to go twice! My wife was only thinking you might drop the money . . ."

As David took the piece of paper money he was offered, he looked the man straight in the face. "Will you look after my bundle while I go? Then I can carry the can better . . ."

Both the man and the woman went red in the face, and David set off without waiting for an answer. They were ashamed of themselves, and that was all David wanted. He had never taken anything he knew belonged to someone else—only fruit growing on trees and bushes and things he found. One had no right to take other people's possessions: that he was sure of . . . Suppose somebody took his bundle!

When the woman had accused him of wanting to take their money, his first impulse had been to walk away. But they had to have petrol, and it was a more telling gesture to leave them his bundle to look after. It was like saying to them, "You think I want to steal from you; but I am David, and since that's what you think, I'm leaving my bundle behind to show you that I think better of you than you do of me." And they understood what he meant, too: he could tell that from their faces.

When they heard up at the filling station in the village that it was an American car that had run out of petrol, they insisted upon driving down themselves with enough to fill the tank, and as David had to return anyway to fetch his bundle, they took him with them in their Vespa.

David handed the American his unused money and, taking his bundle, turned to go.

"Wait a bit, boy. You must have something for your trouble."

David would have been only too glad to accept something from them: he was in desperate need of money to buy a loaf of bread for the next day. But he could not bring himself to take it now. He wanted to earn his money, not just have it given to him. But he did not want to earn it from someone he did not like.

"No, thank you," he said firmly. "I like to earn money sometimes, but only when I want to. I don't need any today."

That was not true, but it felt good to say so. It was like saying, "I am David and I make my own decisions, and no one has any right to tell me what to do."

He ran off in the dusk away from the road and pretended not to hear the American calling him to come back.

He was very hungry when he awoke the next morning. He was in need of water, too, for he had only a few drops. He had left the last village of the evening before some way behind him, but he could see another, a somewhat bigger place, down in the valley. He might be able to earn some money there, but he was by no means certain of it. The evening was the best time to earn money, and the best time to be in town, too, because he could then escape quickly into the shelter of the darkness.

But today he would have to go into town in daylight: he could not wait until evening to get more water. He opened his bundle to drink what was left.

At the bottom of his bundle he found a strange box, the sort used for cigarettes. And in the box there was money—more money than David had ever seen . . . two thousand lire!

One lira was not very much; you could get practically nothing for one lira—but two thousand! As well as the money, there was something written on a slip of paper. A letter . . . David had never had a letter, and he almost wished he did not have one now, for he found it very difficult to read hand-writing, and he had never tried reading English.

But he would not give up. There was such a terrible lot he did not know, and if he did not do something about it, he would go on being just as stupid and ignorant as he had been in the camp. And then he would be caught. You had to help yourself, you had to find out things, or you could not succeed.

After an hour he was fairly sure he knew what was in the letter. It was the American man who had written it, and he said he was quite sure David would not accept money and so he had hidden it in his bundle. He also said they were sorry they had thought he might steal. "Not all strange boys are honest, you know," wrote the American, "but we are sorry we suspected an honest boy. We did not mean you to understand what we said, and we would be glad if you would make use of this money to show you have no hard feelings toward us." And then came a name that David could not read.

David's first thought was that he would now be able to buy a new cake of soap. He had money for bread for many days, and there would still be enough for soap—and perhaps a comb, too!

He told himself that he must not be greedy. Johannes had not liked people to be greedy, and it would be a good thing to keep some of the money to purchase more bread later on . . . He would buy soap, and perhaps one or two other things, but no more. And he would not be in a hurry; he would first consider carefully what he most needed.

The result was that he bought a loaf of bread, a cake of soap, and a comb. Combing his hair was painful, for no one in the camp had had a comb for a very long time, and David's hair had not been combed since. He looked into his mirror to see what he looked like. His hair had a slight wave; he was glad of that because most people here in Italy had wavy hair. But it looked as if it were growing lighter in color. And it was very long.

David reflected seriously, and then he bought himself a pair of scissors and a pencil and a small pad of notepaper as well: the scissors to cut his hair with so that he would not look out of place, and the pencil and paper because for many days now he had wished he could write. Johannes had begun to teach him once; perhaps if he could practice, he could learn to do it properly. It might stand him in good stead to be able to write—one never knew when it might prove useful.

He was not used to having more money than the

price of a loaf of bread, and he found his unexpected wealth a problem. He had now spent almost half of it—the scissors had been expensive. Still, he would have enough to buy bread for some days to come, and he had a great desire to try some cheese. If he could get a bit for fifty lire . . .

It tasted good, even better than he remembered it: he had had it once in the camp and again in the truck on the road to Salonika. When he had satisfied his hunger, he began cutting his hair. He was sitting under an olive tree so bent that it very nearly touched the ground, and he placed his mirror on the lowest branch so that it leaned up against the trunk. Cutting the tufts at the back of his neck where he could not see what he was doing proved a tricky business, but at length he was satisfied with the result.

He wondered if he dared try out his plan of getting a lift. If he chose one of those trucks that carried foodstuffs . . . *they* never drove them.

But every time a truck approached, he lacked the courage to try, although he had made up his mind to do it. He was so frightened that he could feel his heart beat faster and his throat grow tight. Then he thought of God.

"God of the green pastures and the still waters," he said softly, "I am David. And I'm frightened . . . not just ordinary fear that you always have—worse than that. I want to beg a lift so that I can get quickly to another country, but I daren't. If You're strong enough to do something about what people think and feel right inside themselves, then will You please take this fear from me, just long enough for me to wave to a truck? And if it isn't greedy to ask for two things at once, will You let it be a good man that comes in the next one? I haven't yet found anything I can do for You. I am David. Amen."

It seemed that God was strong enough, for when the next truck came along, David was no longer too frightened to get up and step into the roadway.

The truck driver looked exactly like the sailor who had helped him aboard the ship! David waved, the man pulled up and asked where he was going, and David answered, "To Perugia," as he had decided he would when he formed his plan. Perugia was a long way—it would take him three days to walk there.

And so there he was, sitting in the truck by the side of the stranger who was so like the sailor. When he had once told his tale about the circus, the man asked him no questions at all, obviously preferring to do the talking himself. He was called Angelo, and he told David a great deal about his home and family. He had both a father and a mother and many brothers and sisters, and then there was a woman called Rita whom he wanted to marry when he had saved enough money to buy a truck of his own. But his father wanted him to marry someone called Clorinda, and her father had a vineyard.

He talked about it for a long time, as if he were not sure which of them he should marry, and he asked David what he thought.

David considered the matter. "Are they both good people?" he asked finally. "For if there's any difference, you see, I think you'd better marry the one that's good and kind. You could buy a vineyard yourself perhaps when you've earned enough money . . . But I think you've got to decide for yourself. Perhaps your father hasn't thought whether they're kind. You must make quite sure about it before you choose."

Angelo frowned—then he smiled and nodded. "I think you're a very clever boy," he said. "I'll do what you say . . ."

Then he chatted on about his plans for the future, and David listened, but not with the same attention as before. Angelo was stupid. He was a good man, but he *was* stupid. David was puzzled, for he had always thought that good people must be clever. He thought about it for a long time. Could he have been mistaken? He knew so little about anything. But no, Angelo was a grown man, and here was one thing he was quite free to decide for himself, and yet he was ready to let others make up his mind for him—that could only be stupidity.

When they had been driving for several hours, Angelo pulled up and shared his food with David— he gave him a drink from his bottle of wine as well—and a little later they came to Perugia. It was a large town situated on the top of a hill—and there was a very big church that could be seen from the road. David asked to be put down partway up the hill, and when Angelo had driven on, he walked back to the point where the main road continued into the countryside. He had no need of either bread or water, and unless he had to be in a town during the daytime, he preferred to remain in the open.

His plan to stop a truck and ask for a lift had gone off very well. Perhaps he would stop another the next day—provided he were not too frightened. But he would have to do it on his own; since he had not found anything he could do in return, he could not go on asking God for things—it would be greedy, and God might very soon grow tired of a boy who was always frightened and could never do anything for himself. And suppose He grew tired of him the very day something happened that David could not possibly deal with by himself!

David did not know that the very next day something would happen that he could not tackle alone and he still would not ask for help . . .

4

David had never seen a forest before. He had had
a lift that morning and come a long way by car, and
although he wanted to waste no time, he thought he
might spend an hour or two finding out what a forest
looked like. He liked it at first, but after a while he
began to feel uneasy. You could hide behind the
tree trunks . . . and so could *they*!

He realized well enough that *they* were not likely
to wander about a forest just in case they might
find someone. *They* always knew whom they were
after—and even if they were looking for *him*, they
would not be hiding in a forest on the off-chance
that he might pass by. Nevertheless, he felt more
at ease when he was out in the open again. David
preferred places where he could see what was coming far enough ahead for him to hide if he felt suspicious.

He could not yet make up his mind whether *they*

were really after him or not. If they were, it was not because he knew anything. Johannes had always said, every time a new prisoner entered the camp, "Don't tell the boy anything *they* may try to worm out of him afterward." Later on, when Johannes was dead, others had said the same thing. And the man had known that. But there was always the possibility that he was a useful hostage: suppose, for example, he had had a father and that father had been *their* enemy, then they might have threatened him with the fact that they had David in their power.

Not that David really believed it could be so; he could not imagine ever having had a father. But he had to reckon with the possibility that there was *some* reason that made it necessary for them to find him, and that was as near as he could get.

He was suddenly aware of a strange sound. He looked quickly around and threw himself down behind a clump of bushes. There he was again, walking along and thinking without even looking where he was going! There was a house close by. He could see it among the trees . . . a large house and beautiful to look at, almost like a church.

What was that sound? It was strange . . . yes, and wonderful, too!

When he was in Naples, he had seen a balloon. If you could turn into a balloon, that sound was what you might feel like . . . as if you had a great space inside you and it was all filled with air, a heavenly air full of sweet voices that made you fly up and up and your heart beat faster and faster . . . not be cause you were afraid, but because you were . . happy? Was that what happiness felt like?

David knew he was listening to music. There had once been a musician in the camp, and before he had been there long enough to lapse into silence, he had talked about music and tried to explain what it sounded like. But David had not understood.

He understood now, however. That sound that seemed to flood right into your very being and draw you upward and upward—that was all the instruments playing together . . . And that thin, delicate sound that made your heart beat so fast—that must be the violin! . . . One morning by the side of a little stream he had found a red flower. A drop of water had fallen onto its red petals, and a ray of sunshine had caught it and made it tremble on the flower in David's hand and glisten with many colors . . . And David thought that if a ray of light from the sun could have made a drop of water speak, its voice would have been like the clearest notes of the violin . . .

"What the devil! . . . You young thief, forcing

your way into people's grounds in broad daylight! I'll show you, you . . . Come here and I'll give you a good hiding!"

The voice fell like an explosion on David's ears. The wonderful sound of the music lay murdered, crushed, and kicked to death by an evil voice . . . He just managed to catch sight of a boy, a black-haired boy with spiteful, ill-natured eyes, before he was knocked down and trying to ward off the blows. It was impossible to get away, for the boy was as big as himself, and to escape would mean hitting back. David shielded his head against the boy's kicks and clenched his teeth. The blows began to lose some of their force, and the boy seemed to hesitate.

"So you won't hit back, eh? Scared to fight, I suppose?"

David did not answer, and the boy set about him again but less violently this time—rather as if he felt he had to.

"Use your fists, you young swine!"

"No."

The boy appeared to have grown tired of striking him, at least for the moment, and David sat up with blood streaming from his nose.

"You seem to enjoy a good hiding. Maybe you

like me for giving you one!" The boy's voice was provocative.

David regarded him calmly. "No, I don't. I hate you—and I'd hate you just as much if it had been anyone else you'd hit. I wouldn't care if you fell dead right now; at least I'd be sure you'd never look at anything beautiful again!"

The strange boy looked astonished. "Why don't you fight then?" he asked crossly.

"Because if I hit you back, I'd be no better than you are. I'd be just as rotten and worthless, and I'd have no right to be free!"

The strange boy grinned at him, but there was a look of uncertainty about him, and his eyes shifted uneasily. "You're not all there!" he said. "Who do you think you're talking to?"

"I don't think. I know. I'm talking to someone who likes using brute force. And that's why I don't want to talk to you anymore . . . You can hit me again if you can catch me!"

With that David jumped up smartly and ran off. He could not run very quickly because he was beginning to ache all over where the other boy had struck him. But the strange boy did not follow him: he only shouted, "Idiot! You're a crazy coward!"

David had the impression that he was shouting loudly for his own benefit.

David was sick, and every time he thought about the young stranger, he felt like being sick again. He found it difficult to understand that people who were well off here in Italy, where they had so much food to eat and were surrounded by such beauty of sea and countryside, could still love violence. That boy was just like the guards in the camp, the only difference being that the guards did not leave off striking till their victims lost consciousness. The boy, of course, had had only his bare hands to strike with and had tired of the effort too soon.

For a moment David was tempted to think that perhaps there were no good people at all outside concentration camps, but then he reminded himself of the sailor and Angelo and the English people who might have been ignorant but were certainly not bad. And then when he was living among the rocks overhanging the sea, there had been the man with the loaves. He had not been bad either; he just had not been brave enough to let a boy go without giving him away—not for more than a few days, at any rate.

Yes, he felt there must be somewhere where everybody was kind and decent, a free country where people did not believe violence was a good thing. And he would find a free country—if he could do it before he was caught again. But first of all he must have a thorough wash. He thought from the lay of the land that there was probably a river nearby.

There was—a large one, too, although it was partly dried up as rivers usually were in the summertime. David took his clothes off and put them in the water. He scrubbed himself thoroughly all over. His soap would soon be worn thin at that rate, but he did not care—he must not leave a spot unwashed where the boy had touched him. Not until all contact with him had been washed away would David be able to feel free again.

He washed his hair, too, and then took his clothes out of the water and spread them to dry. He lay down beside them and made an effort to calm himself and forget the boy. Much better to recall what the music had sounded like . . . Had there been a large orchestra inside that fine house or had it been a radio?

He was startled by the sound of voices not far away. He pulled his wet clothes toward him. A large boulder provided good cover on one side, and in front of him the trunk of an olive and rows of close-growing vines, old and gnarled, completely hid him from view when he ducked down.

It was some children playing, and David decided he would watch them. He usually hurried away when he saw children; he was afraid of them. He had never spoken to children, and he did not know how to begin. From the very first day when he had made his home among the rocks, he had made up his mind to avoid children: they were much more dangerous than grown-ups—except *them*, of course. They were more dangerous because it was easier for them to see how different he was. Grown-ups could not really remember what children were like, so Johannes had once said. But other children would very soon discover that he knew nothing of the things they took for granted. One thing alone would give him away: he had no idea how to play. People were always talking about children playing, but playing seemed to mean so many different things that David had given up trying to find out what it was.

There were so many more important things to learn about, and as long as he avoided children, there was no need for him to be able to play.

But since he could not get away now until they left, he might just as well watch them. He parted the vines cautiously so that he could see.

There were two little boys, much smaller than himself, and a girl who was somewhat bigger, though still quite young. Shouting and laughing and all three talking at once, they were running around a small building—not the sort of place people lived in but where they kept tools and wheelbarrows and baskets for fruit picking.

David could not take his eyes off the girl. She had black curly hair, very long and tied with a red ribbon, and everything about her was beautiful—not just her fine red dress, but everything . . . Her laughter sounded like the light tinkling of polished glass, and when she moved, she reminded David of a flower swaying in the wind.

They said they were going to play something they called Davy Crockett and the Indians. First the little boys were to be Indians. They would capture the girl, shut her up in the shed, and go off. Then when they came back, they would pretend to be Davy Crockett and set her free.

David thought it sounded silly . . . but that was probably because he did not really know what ordinary children were like. As far as he was concerned, he had no desire to be anyone but himself. He might feel differently about other things—like wanting to stay free long enough to find a country where he could live in safety—but he would always want to be David. That was why he had determined to go on living that morning he had come across his rock. As long as he had been a prisoner in the concentration camp, he had not cared what happened to him. He had followed the others' example and done as he was told, but that had not been living. But from that morning when he first fully realized he was an individual person called David, free and able to think for himself, everything had been different. No, David felt quite sure he would never pretend to be anyone else.

The girl had gone into the shed now, and so there was nothing more to watch. He was very tired, too, and thought he might just as well take a nap before the little boys returned and they all went off and left him free to go on his way.

David was awakened by shouting and crying . . . and a strange smell in the air.

"It's on fire! It's on fire! It's all your fault, Cecha—you thought of it! You know very well we aren't allowed to play with fire . . . ."

It was the two little boys. And it was the shed that was on fire!

"What shall we do? Run and get Carlo, Cecha . . . Oh, if only she doesn't get burned up while you're gone . . . ."

Both the little boys were crying. One of them set off running in the direction David had come from; the other just stood there and wept.

She was burning . . . the girl! It was the girl they were talking about now—the little girl who looked so like a flower was inside that fire!

David sprang up and took a step forward; then he turned around and, grabbing his clothes, flung them into the river and jumped in after them. They were now sopping wet again . . .

So many thoughts flashed through his mind as he ran that it seemed like hours to David before he reached the shed. A man in the camp had once escaped from a burning building by wrapping wet clothes around his head to keep the smoke out and prevent himself from losing consciousness, and he had not been burned about the face . . . If only he could get her out now; the shed wall was no longer burning so fiercely, but the door was a regular bonfire. And all those dry leaves and stalks the roof was made of—he would have to have her out before the fire got a proper hold on them . . .

He was just going to call on God to help him when a thought occurred to him. God certainly would not want that little girl, so like a flower and so beautiful to look at, to die. Here, then, was something he could do for God in return!

He could not say it aloud because he was running too hard, and so he said it to himself: "God of the green pastures and the still waters, please don't help me. I want to do it by myself so that You'll know I've found something I can do for You . . . I am David. Amen."

By that time he had reached the burning shed. The little boy who had stayed behind was still crying . . . and David could hear other voices down by the river, but he had no time to look around. With all the speed he could muster, he undid his bundle and took out his knife, picked up his wet clothes again and with one hand held his trousers up in front of his nose and mouth. Then he sprang into the blazing fire.

The flames had hardly reached the inside, but it was full of smoke. In the middle of the floor sat the little girl tied to an old chair. Tears were streaming from her eyes, and between fits of coughing she was shouting hoarsely for help.

David's first impulse was to run straight to her . . . Then he realized he must stop to consider what to do. He must think quickly but as carefully as if he had all the time in the world. He must have time to cut through her bonds; yet the blaze from the door was now beginning to spread rapidly, the flames licking along the floor where dry leaves lay by the wall. There were no windows in the shed . . . They would have to get out again through the burning doorway. Near it stood a pile of baskets and boxes, which David removed as far from the door as he could, leaving a train of three or four pieces of wood behind him. Then he seized a birch broom, already smoldering slightly, and swept all the dry leaves away from the other walls toward the pile of baskets so that, as he hoped, the fire would be encouraged to burn in that direction instead of filling the whole room at once.

In the meantime, he was coughing, too, for he could not hold his wet clothes up to his face and shift the baskets and sweep the floor at the same time.

Next, he turned his attention to the girl. "Shut your eyes," he said. "And your mouth." he wound his wet shirt around her face, taking care that she could breathe freely inside it. Then he started cutting through her bonds. Luckily they were only a coarse loose twine. If *they* had bound her to the chair, it would not have been so easy! . . . But the knife was not very sharp, and he had to saw backward and forward several times, and the little girl was beginning to wriggle her feet. David gripped them firmly to show her she must sit still . . . he dared not speak and risk getting more smoke inside his lungs. The heat was quite unbearable, but he was going to do it, and he was *going* to . . . he *must*!

The cords were cut through at last. The little girl rose unsteadily to her feet and pulled the shirt from her face. Their eyes were hot and smarting, and they had to blink all the time . . . but David saw she was looking at him . . . with such big black eyes. Then she shut them and stumbled and would have fallen if David had not taken hold of her. She had fainted. That meant she could not run out with him; he would have to carry her.

For one moment David felt he had promised God too much . . . he would not be able to do it. Perhaps she had died from the smoke . . . He laid her down on the floor and put his ear to her chest, as the men in the camp had always done to see if one of their fellows was still alive. He could hear her heart beating.

David wound his shirt about her head again and pulled his trousers down over his own. They were well worn, and so it was easy enough to stick his fingers through a hole and make it bigger. He would have to see where the door was . . . If he could not carry her through the fire, he would throw her clear. He would be able to manage that much before he succumbed to the flames. He was terrified of being burned to death, but perhaps it would be over quickly, almost as quickly as being shot. It would be better not to think about it at the moment; he must concentrate on getting her up again and trying to run. She was heavy . . . It was a good thing she was not as big as himself, for if she had been, he could not have done it. For a split second David hesitated in front of the raging, crackling fire that had been a door. Then he made straight for it.

And then it was all over. He had gotten through and he had the little girl with him. He could not remember afterward the order in which things happened. There were the two small boys outside and several other people as well, two especially who were bigger . . . He was overcome with coughing and would certainly have fallen if he had not had the little girl to look after . . . The others shouted and wanted to take her, but he pushed them aside, and seating himself and the little girl on the ground, freed both their faces from his clothes. They were scarcely even damp now.

Then he discovered that the little girl's hair had caught fire; one of her long curls had hung outside his shirt . . . So the fire thought it would cheat him of his prize! David failed to hear a car draw up, nor did he hear his own shout of anger. He cast his clothes aside and, seizing the little girl's hair in both hands, squeezed it tight, smothering the fire, not even aware that he was burning himself. The flames were nearly out, and he pressed her head against his chest to destroy the last sparks in case the fire should still be lurking there in the hope that he would let it have her . . . Then he had another fit of coughing and in a daze wiped his eyes with his free hand. Then he looked down at the black curly head again. No, the fire was all out now . . . and it had not touched the little girl, apart from her hair.

She was on the point of coming around, as he could see from the slight flutter of her eyelids. But David continued to hold her . . . as if he were much too tired to think about setting her down. He just sat there, conscious only of the fact that he had beaten the fire and kept his promise. The little girl who looked like a flower was still alive. She opened her eyes, and they looked straight into David's wonderingly, not as if she were afraid but as if she were now quite sure that everything was all right.

"Who are you?" she asked.

Not "Where do you come from?" or "What are you called?" or "What do you want?"—the questions people generally asked him—but "Who are you?"

"I am David."

Her lashes were enormously long. They shone black and lustrous as if the sun were shining on them, and the skin of her face looked as delicate as the petals of a flower. She was smiling now, only slightly, but enough to show a gleam of small white teeth between her red lips. David felt something happen inside him . . . as if he heard music . . . something wonderful. And something happened to his face, too, a movement that took him by surprise.

"David?" repeated the little girl, not as if she had not heard him but rather as if the sound of his name were something good to hold on to. And she did not stop smiling.

Then David understood. He was smiling himself now.

"Yes," he said.

One of those who were standing near them and whom David had not noticed before was drying his eyes; and it was not one of the little boys, it was a grown man. But it was a familiar voice that he finally heard, a voice that said, "And I said you were a crazy coward! I've never before seen anyone do such a brave thing . . . Father, you didn't see what happened . . . The two littl'uns had tied her up, and he went right through the burning doorway and cut her free and carried her out again through the fire . . ."

"Yes, I saw him coming out, Carlo . . . He's saved Maria's life . . . and only just in the nick of time. Look, the roof's caught fire now . . . We would have been too late, Carlo. If he hadn't been here, Maria would have been lost."

"Even if I'd been here in plenty of time, I don't

think I'd have dared . . . and I . . . Father, I chased him off this afternoon . . ."

"The boy's burned, Father. Look, his arms and legs are all black, and he's got no clothes . . ." It was one of the little boys who had at length stopped crying.

David heard their voices from far away. He could not bring himself to take his eyes off the little girl's face, for he knew it was she who had made him smile . . . And suppose his smile went when he stopped looking at her; then he would never find out how one came to smile. One smiled for joy, of course! Or was it happiness? Johannes had said there was a difference . . . Joy passed, but happiness never completely disappeared; a touch of it would always remain to remind one it had been there. It was happiness that made one smile, then. He would always remember that.

So David sat there on the ground, burned and black with soot, stark naked but full of happiness and triumph, clinging to the prize he had cheated death of. He had done what he said he would do . . . He, David, had promised God he would give Him the little girl, all by himself and without help—and he had done it. And God was clearly pleased with his gift—had He not immediately shown him how to smile? And the little girl who was so beautiful and soft to touch—she did not ask a lot of questions; she seemed quite satisfied that he was David.

Yes, God obviously thought the gift a good one.

"Shall I carry her for you, David?"

David looked up, startled. The man who was the children's father was smiling at him. But he was not holding out his hands to take the little girl. He seemed to understand that she now belonged to David who had rescued her from the fire . . . and he would not take her without permission.

David noticed at once how painful his hands were and how dreadfully tired he was. "Yes, please," he said.

The little girl resisted slightly, and as soon as her father had lifted her up so that she could no longer see David, she called out, "David . . ."

David began to get up, and the ill-natured boy who was called Carlo stepped toward him as if to help him to his feet. He did not look ill-natured now, but David drew back from his touch and stood up by himself.

"You needn't be frightened, you know," Carlo said eagerly. "I didn't know, you see . . . I think you're the bravest boy I've ever seen and I'm terribly sorry I . . . gave you a beating . . . I'm sorry . . ."

"I'm not frightened," said David curtly. Then

he moved away to where the little girl could see him and said, "I'll go with you to the car . . ."

The girl smiled again and held out her hand. David hesitated and then took it in his own. "David's hand hurts him, Maria," said her father. But the little girl did not let go. She tightened her grip a little so that David had to go with her. Then she raised his hand and pressed it to her cheek. "David," she said.

David could feel himself smiling again, and he wondered whether smiling was something you could not help, something that happened of its own accord . . . When they had driven off, he would see if he could make himself smile by thinking of the way the little girl looked . . . as if she were a flower and as if she were pleased he was David.

But they would not let him go. None of them would, neither the two little boys who were carrying his clothes between them, nor the two big ones, Carlo and the other who was called Andrea. And their father said there could be no question about it. David must go home with them.

David tried to explain that he had to be on his way, but when he held out his hand for his clothes, the two little ones started jumping around him, laughing and shouting, "You can't have 'em! You can't have 'em! Not before you come home with us!".

The boy who was called Andrea laughed, too, and slung David's bundle across his shoulders.

David began to grow angry. They might be glad he had rescued the little girl from the fire, but that gave them no right to tell him what to do—nobody had any right to do that!

Then the children's father said, "My name's Giovanni di Levana del 'Varchi, and these are my children, Andrea and Carlo, the two little ones, Cecha and Guglio, and, of course, Maria . . . We shan't keep you long if you must go on, but you mustn't deny me the pleasure of thanking you properly for what you've done. And what do you suppose Maria's mother would say if I let you go without giving her a chance to thank you for saving Maria's life? Unless we . . . no, David, you mustn't ask me to do that . . ."

David's anger vanished. They did not want to tell him what to do; they were only asking him to do something for them . . . to give them pleasure. He could not spoil their pleasure.

The man with the long name was smiling at him, but David could not manage to smile back; he could do it only when he was looking at the little girl. So instead he said earnestly, "I won't ask you to do anything, and, of course, I'll do as you wish, signor."

He put out his hand for his clothes again, and this time the boys gave them to him, but their father said hastily, "No, boys, let David have the traveling rug from the backseat to wrap around him. It's softer and won't irritate his burns so much . . ."

David looked at the beautiful rug anxiously; it was a check pattern in many different colors. "But I'm black from the fire, signor. I shall make it dirty . . ."

The children all cried out that it did not matter in the least, and so David was wrapped carefully in the traveling rug and helped onto the front seat next to Maria, who snuggled up to him although it was a wide seat with plenty of room on it.

Luckily he had hit upon a new name for the place where the circus was supposed to be, for the boys inundated him with questions until their father told them to leave David in peace.

They drove through a tall gateway and found themselves in a garden so big that it seemed to have no end, and the house where the children lived was the same magnificent house that David had seen earlier that afternoon.

David thought as quick as lightning that a house was dangerous. But then they were glad he had rescued the girl. As long as they did not discover where he came from, they certainly would not wish him any harm. And it would be an enormous advantage to find out what a house was like inside. Nevertheless, as David walked up the broad flight of steps in his bare feet and stepped over the threshold with its magnificently carved door, he felt a vague disquiet. What would happen there? Nothing to harm him—but something all the same . . . something different from what he was used to, something he had not expected or even knew existed. David could not explain why he felt ill at ease and thrust the thought aside. He had done it now—he had entered a house.

He was confused by so many impressions that he could not grasp anything properly at first. The house was full of things, and there were women in black dresses and white aprons who must be maids. And there was a very beautiful woman who turned out to be the children's mother, and she laughed and cried almost in the same breath, and it was very difficult to escape her caresses . . . And then they phoned for a doctor, and David said he would like to wash, but they would not let him—not before the doctor had been there, they said, for he must not get water on his burns, and it was no use David's saying he did not think he was very badly burned.

Then the doctor came and said David was right.

Maria had come to no harm at all because David had carried her so quickly through the fire. David could thank the thick soles of his feet, he said, that he had gotten off so lightly from his act of heroism. He was a little burned about the hands and arms and legs, but it would not be long before he recovered.

David knew that doctors were good men—they were never allowed inside the camp—and the other prisoners had always told him that doctors were there to help people when they were ill. So he submitted quietly while the doctor touched him and wiped the dirt away with something from a bottle. It hurt all the time, and then the doctor put something else on his burns, and that hurt, too. But the doctor explained that if he did not do it, the burns would be more painful the next day. David must just go to sleep now, and then he would feel better when he woke up again.

The doctor was right, too. David did feel better. He felt fine, in fact, although his hands were still rather painful. He opened his eyes and remembered that he was lying in a bed! He shifted his position slightly, but the bed still felt cozy and wonderfully soft. He sat up to see what it was like, and the bed gave under his weight and bounced gently under him. So that was what a bed was . . . a big box on legs, made of dark polished wood . . . with . . . with pillows and sheets.

Yes, it was going to be most interesting to see what a house looked like! And he thought of all the words he would now be able to use. He knew many words he had never used because he was afraid that, not knowing the things they referred to, he might use them wrongly and show his ignorance. Besides, he would have felt silly saying words without really knowing what they meant. Sheets. Imagine sleeping every night in a soft bed like that where you did not feel cold . . . and between soft white sheets where you knew everything around you was perfectly clean!

He continued gazing at the sheets for a while longer. He was itching with impatience to examine the room and everything in it, but there was something he had to attend to first. He had learned what happiness meant and he had found out how to smile—without even practicing in a mirror! That was a very important thing—much more important than the bed, for he could not take that with him, but the other—that would stay with him wherever he went.

Johannes had taught him always to remember to say thank you. He had meant to people, of course, and he had been very strict about it. He had insisted upon David's saying thank you even to *them*—when they gave him food, for example. David had not wanted to . . . not to *them*. But Johannes had said, "Politeness is something you owe other people, because when you show a little courtesy, everything becomes easier and better. But first and foremost, it's something you owe yourself. You are David. And if you never allow other people to influence what you're really like, then you've something no one can take from you—not even *they*. Never mind what others are like—you must still be David. Do you understand what I mean?"

David had not said "yes" right away, for Johannes would always have him think carefully first and not answer until he understood what he was saying. But afterward David had realized something of what Johannes had meant . . . especially when, a short time later, there appeared in the camp an inspector who thought David might know something about Johannes. "The boy knows nothing," the man had said, and he had been right, of course. But if he had known anything *they* wanted to find out, he would still have done his best to say nothing, even if *they* had offered him extra food to talk and even though Johannes would never have scolded him for doing it. He would have tried to keep silent, not because of anything other people might say or do, but simply because he was David and Johannes' friend.

After that he had always said thank you when he was given food—not to make *them* think he did not hate them, but so that they could see he was polite because *he* wanted to be.

And if you wanted to be polite to people—even to *them*—then you must also remember to be polite to God. It would not take more than a minute, and he could examine the room afterward.

David stared hard at the sheet so that nothing in the room should distract his attention, and then said quickly, "God of the green pastures and the still waters, I want to thank You because I've learned about happiness and found out how to smile. And thank You, too, for being pleased I rescued the girl for You. I hope I can find something different to do for You next time, because that was very difficult and I was very frightened of the fire, and so I would rather not do anything like that too often. Will You please let it do for the next three times I may need You to help me. I am David. Amen."

As soon as he had said amen, he was out of bed. On the floor was a large patterned carpet, soft and cozy to walk on. Chairs and a table—those he recognized, of course, but he had never seen such magnificent ones—and a large wardrobe and a piece of furniture with drawers in it; it was not a writing table . . . a chest of drawers, perhaps. And everything was elaborately carved in designs of leaves and fruit and animals' heads. The window was wide and tall, and on both sides of it hung curtains of some soft thick material dyed the same color as the leaves of an olive tree.

David moved noiselessly about the room, examining everything closely, touching and returning to look again . . . There was a bowl on the table, and two tall, slender objects that he pondered over deeply till he came to the conclusion that they must be candlesticks. They were shiny . . . silver? Yes, they must be silver. David repeated the word slowly to himself, enjoying the sound of it. Silver was something very rich and fine. They looked like silver, at least from what David had heard about it.

His glance traveled upward. There was a picture! Not the sort you saw pasted on the outside walls of shops and houses, but one that showed a beautiful scene. David stood on the bed and stretched up to see it better. It was a painting. He was sure of it. It was just like what the men in the camp had described to him.

David sat down in bed quite overcome. If only he could remember it all! He had been so small when he had any knowledge of what the world was like outside the concentration camp. And Johannes had not liked the men to tell him too much about it. "What the boy doesn't know, he won't miss," he would say. David had once heard him say that when they thought he had fallen asleep. They had always answered his questions, but they would leave it at that, and afterward, when Johannes was dead, he had spoken to no one.

He was lucky, therefore, to have learned at least something, and now it was up to him to remember all he could and keep his eyes open so that the children and their parents would not discover how little he really did know.

He wondered whether he should stay where he was until someone came and said he might go downstairs. Or should he just get up and go down? But his clothes were not there, and he could not walk about the house with nothing on.

Before he had time to consider further, the door opened gently and the children's mother peeped in.

"So you're awake," she said, smiling. "I've brought you some clothes in case you want to get up. You may stay in bed if you'd rather . . . Are your hands still painful? And your ankles—are they any worse?"

David answered that his ankles hurt most, but

he was not in great pain anywhere and would like to get up. "But they're not my clothes," he said as he saw what the children's mother was laying across the chair.

"No, they're being washed. These are Andrea's, but I think they'll fit you."

David looked at them anxiously. "I might tear them on a branch," he said.

"My dear boy, and after all you've done for us!"

David wondered if he should explain that he had not rescued the little girl on their account but entirely for his own sake in order to repay his debt to God. He decided not to, however; perhaps she would not understand, and perhaps she did not know about his God of the green pastures and still waters. It was safer not to say too much, for then he would avoid saying anything that might rouse their suspicions of him.

He put the clothes on—or rather, the children's mother helped him to, for they were very fine clothes with buttons and a thing called a zipper, which David was not at all sure how to manage. There were trousers, short brown ones like those the children had been wearing, and a shirt—not one like his own but a real shirt with buttons. It was green. There were stockings, too, and the kind of shoes they called sandals . . . David had never tried wearing anything on his feet before. And there were pockets in the trousers . . .

David stood quite still, and his eyes began to feel hot, as if he wanted to cry. He had never thought he would wear clothes like these, and he had an irrepressible desire to see what he looked like, to see whether he looked like an ordinary boy at last.

The lady seemed to guess what was passing through his mind, for she opened the wardrobe door, and there on the inside was a large full-length mirror.

It was big enough for a boy to see himself from top to toe . . . or for a grown man, come to that. David regarded himself critically. He did not think there was anything odd about what he saw. True, he did not have black hair, but otherwise he looked like any other boy who was not particularly fat. And he had grown quite brown from being in the sun so much.

Without thinking, he said, "I look quite like an ordinary boy now, don't I?"

"Of course you do," she answered, but she did not sound as if she altogether meant it. Then she added, "And you look a very handsome boy, and a brave one, too. Come, the children are impatient to see you, and you must be hungry . . ."

She walked so quickly that David could not see

anything properly. He was aware that there was furniture everywhere, and carpets and paintings, but he had no opportunity to see what they looked like. They descended a long broad staircase and came to other rooms. One of them had a door that led out to the large garden, and there they found the children and their father. Maria was looking rather pale, but her father said she had insisted upon getting up and coming downstairs so that she could see David again.

David found himself smiling once more as he looked at her.

"Drink your milk now, children, and then you can take David out to play—but not too roughly, mind; you must be careful of his burns."

They said he should stay with them for a while, at any rate until his arms and legs were quite well again, and he was welcome to stay even longer if he were not expected back with the circus immediately.

David did not really know what he would rather do. He wanted to go, but at the same time he wanted to stay in order to learn all he could about the house.

He looked up intently at the children's father and mother; they were both smiling. "Can I go now, this very moment, if I want to?"

The children's father stopped smiling and looked

disappointed. "Yes, of course, David, if that's what you'd rather do. But we should all be very glad if you would stay with us for a while so that we could show you how grateful we are."

David considered. If only it were not too dangerous, he would like to stay with them a little and learn more about their way of life. "If I can go whenever I want to, then I'd like to stay for a bit," he said at length. "Yes, thank you. I don't have to join the circus just yet. But please don't be so grateful, for you see I *wanted* to rescue the little girl from the fire, and you've already thanked me."

"Yes, but we shall continue to be grateful to you as long as we live, David. It's something we shall never forget," the children's father said quietly.

David felt very, very tired that evening. He was to sleep once more in that soft cozy bed, and yet it was a long time before he fell asleep, so excited was he with all he had seen that day . . . He could not remember even half of it: there was not room in his head for so many new impressions at once. But he did remember the food. Never would he forget what it was like to eat in such a house—it was almost like listening to music!

Johannes had once told him about it, and when he saw it, he remembered. One of the prisoners had made some remark about eating like pigs, and so David had asked whether people ate differently outside the camp.

But he had never been able to picture what it was like, and now he had seen for himself. You sat at a table covered with a cloth so white that it gleamed. And there were plates—one for each person—with flowers painted on them, and candlesticks with candles in them and flowers in a bowl. And the glasses you drank from were fine and delicate and tinkled if you happened to touch them with a knife or fork. And the knives and forks and spoons were all of silver, and everyone had his own, as well as a napkin to wipe his fingers on should they become greasy. David was afraid he would not know how to eat properly, but he watched the children's father and mother first and then did as they did. It was lucky he was used to being careful in his movements, for otherwise he would certainly have spilled something. And there was more food than you could possibly eat at one time—all kinds of different things—and everything tasted wonderful. David dared not eat very much, for he knew the rich food might make him ill since he was not used to it.

But to think of eating as something beautiful! Well, if that was how the prisoners in the concentration camp had been in the habit of eating, he could well understand why they said they ate like pigs there.

The food was brought in by the servants and cleared away before the next course arrived, and you were given clean plates and knives and everything. And the children said they ate like that every day, and several times a day . . .

The next day he would enjoy it all again.

5

David thought living in a house was very difficult. It was not the house itself—that was lovely to be in—but the people. What was so difficult about them was that they constantly seemed to expect him to say and do things he would never have thought of, and what appeared sensible and natural to him seemed to surprise them . . .

Otherwise, being in a house was lovely—quite wonderful. David contemplated the two words with satisfaction, repeating them several times to himself. He had been in the house many days now and was learning all the time. He had learned, for example, to use those two words . . . they meant something that was good. It was satisfying to know several words for the same thing, for then he could describe exactly to what degree a thing was good. It was just the same with the word "beautiful." You could divide it into three: if something were only a little beautiful, it was "nice"; if it were more beautiful, you said "pretty" . . . and finally "beautiful."

Being able to use words properly was a great advantage, for the more words you knew the meaning of, the better you could think. And besides, it was important when you were talking to people: they were not so surprised at what you said if you used the right words. The children's mother had laughed when he saw the bathroom and said it was "beautiful and good." He should have said "lovely," of course.

He would always remember the bathroom with its gleaming pale green tub and all that clear clean water that came when you just turned a faucet. You could have as much hot water as you liked and sit in it right up to your neck. And there was soap, large pieces of it, that smelled much better than the cake he had bought himself. It rubbed into a beautiful soft lather that made you quite, quite clean. And when you had finished, there were large soft clean towels to dry yourself on. And there were little sticks to clean your nails with, and you could brush your teeth . . . David had never tried that before, and the first time he made his mouth sore doing it. But it was wonderful to be so clean.

There were books in the house, too . . . not just one but many. When he had first arrived, the children's father had asked him if there was anything he particularly wanted. David had considered carefully and then said, "I think most of all I'd like a book to read." He wanted to hear music again, too, but the book was more important. He said it must be a book published before 1917. The children's father had smiled and asked why, but David had not dared to tell him it was because he wanted to be sure that what was in it was true and not something *they* had made up.

The meals he had in that house delighted him, both because there was so much to eat and it all tasted so good, and even more because the table looked so beautiful with the glasses and the silver and the white cloth and with a fine plate for everybody.

But people he found difficult . . . They seemed to have no idea of what was good. The children's mother was quite pleased that he liked the bathroom, but the children themselves hated it—at least, the boys did. Perhaps he was wrong, but no matter how hard he tried, he could not help liking it himself. He had nothing against being dirty; you got dirty in the course of the day, and you just could not avoid it. But to be free to wash the dirt off whenever you wanted to . . . yes, that was wonderful! And yet the children did not seem to understand that, and he dared not tell them how disgusting it was when men who had been clean, with clean shiny hair and clean teeth, grew so matted and ingrained with dirt that everything about them smelled repulsive and looked loathsome.

But if he told them that, then of course they might discover where he came from, and then they would be obliged to send for *them*.

The children could not understand either why he was so anxious to read books. They always wanted him to go out with them, and so he had to go, though he longed to be left alone to sit and read his books. There was no end to what you could learn from books if only you had time enough . . . and it took a lot of time. He could read more rapidly now, but not really quickly for all that, and he had first to choose his books. If only he could read all of them! But David knew he did not have very much time: he must go on before winter came. And so it was important for him to read books where he would find information that would be useful to him.

It was, in fact, the books that led him to stay. The people, the children especially, made him nervous—and he hated being in the same place with Carlo. The house he could leave, though not without regret. But it was important to go on reading as long as possible so that he could find out the things he wanted to know, and that was why he had now been there many days.

He had learned that he could never become an ordinary boy. The knowledge was painful, but there was no point in deceiving himself. He would like to have learned to be an ordinary boy, to be as a boy should be outside the concentration camp.

And yet . . . the children were so stupid that David did not understand them at all. He did not understand why they did not like bathing. He did not understand why they preferred to live without knowing anything. They did not seem to think it was necessary, as if there were no difference between a donkey and a human being. David was very fond of donkeys: they were—he sought for the right word—nice. Anything you liked, if it was not really beautiful, you called "nice." But it was very much better to be a human being able to learn things and know things.

He did not understand either why they did not regard mealtimes as gracious occasions. They would often spill things on the white cloth and sit so restlessly and be so clumsy and awkward with their knives and forks that they soon brought disorder to the beautifully arranged table where they had been sitting.

But the most dangerous thing about them was that you could not follow what they were thinking about. They always wanted to be playing, and David had particularly wanted to learn how to play. And he could play a little now. He knew how to play ball. A ball was round and satisfying to hold, and it had colors, good bright colors. He liked throwing it to Andrea and catching it again. Racing with Andrea was good, too, and climbing trees and jumping over a rope, higher and higher . . . He liked the sort of games that made him aware how well his body would obey him. And the sort where you had to make something, turning a few bits of wood into things you could use . . . all that kind of thing.

But the children often wanted to play at being other people. They would pretend one was the grocer, and another would come and buy from him. Or they would be a mother and father and some other children . . . or they might be pirates. That sort of thing David did not care for, and when they said he could choose first what he wanted to be, he would always answer that he would be David who had come to watch them.

Once they had wanted to play a game where some of them had to be soldiers and take the others prisoner. "And I'll be captain over the soldiers!"

shouted Carlo, hastily adding, "That is if you don't want to be, David."

David had looked straight at him. "I will not play anything wicked and horrible," he had replied.

Maria immediately said that if David would not play, she would not either, but Andrea said with some irritation, "You're a strange person, David. What's wicked about that?"

David had waited until he was sure his voice would not tremble. "I'm not very good at playing, but I can see when you play you try to imitate what's real, and I won't have anything to do with pretending to take people prisoner. It's horrible and wicked . . . and no one has any right to take other people prisoner. Everybody has a right to his life and freedom, and anyone who takes them away has lost his own right to be a human being."

"Yes, but David"—Andrea's voice was no longer irritated, only interested—"what if there's a murderer. Shouldn't he be put in prison either? Or a thief, or something like that? There's got to be someone to decide who has to go to prison . . ."

David frowned. "I don't know . . . Yes, a murderer, he should go to prison to stop him murdering more people . . . but you mustn't lay hands on him or starve him . . . I . . . no, I'm not quite sure about it. I haven't found out all about it yet. But no person has any right over other people: a man must be his own master."

"Yes, but Father and Mother have a right over us," Andrea said.

"No, it's not a right . . . at least, I don't think so. It's more of a . . . a duty. I mean, since they're your parents, they must give you food and clothes and teach you all the things you can't know by yourselves, so that you can manage for yourselves when you're grown up. What they do is something good . . . it's not that sort of thing I mean by right over people. Having right over others is something horrible and shameful, using force to make them do what you want."

At that point the two little boys began yawning. "Aren't we going to play anything?" they asked impatiently. "David can decide what we're going to play then."

David had felt relieved. He had to answer Andrea, of course, and try to explain things to him. But Andrea still did not seem to understand what he was driving at, and David was always afraid that if he talked too much, he might be led into saying something he should not. And, anyway, he did not care to talk when Carlo was there. The first couple of days, Carlo had tried to wheedle himself into

David's good books, but David was only too familiar with that kind of approach, and so Carlo had stopped. David spoke to him politely whenever it was necessary, just as he had always done to *them*, but Carlo had by now realized that he could not expect any more of him.

Nevertheless, it was unpleasant. Carlo was so good at deception that you could hardly credit he was only a boy. He had made a great effort to convince David that he was not bad . . . and when he had realized that David was not going to let himself be impressed, he pretended to be hurt by it. David thought what a good thing it was he had seen so much deception in the camp, or he would certainly have been taken in, just as Andrea and the two little boys and Maria were. They did not know Carlo was bad, and that was why David felt uncomfortable in his presence. The two little boys noticed nothing, but David felt that Andrea and Maria knew he hated Carlo and were sorry that he did so.

They said nothing. They were always very kind to him, but that only made matters worse. It would have been better had they been like the two little ones who were too young to notice.

David liked the two little boys, though he did not understand them and felt quite sure he had never been so small himself. But they were cute, rather like two little animals tumbling about noisily, never still for a moment. He knew, too, that if he had been a proper ordinary boy, he would have liked Andrea very much indeed. He was friendly and fair, and when you pointed out that something was beautiful, he could see it was. And he did not ruin things the way Carlo and the two younger ones did. But as it was, it would be dangerous for David to be too friendly with him—he might very likely forget to take care what he said, and then Andrea would think him odd and begin to ask questions.

It was only with Maria that David felt quite at ease. She never left him, and she could always guess when anyone said something to make him uneasy. At such moments she would divert attention from him by saying something herself, or else she would answer for him so that all he had to say was, "Yes, that's what I meant."

And yet he never felt ignorant when he was with her. She wanted to know what he thought about everything, and she never seemed to think him strange. There were many things he could help her with, too, for she was not very strong. And then she was so pretty to look at, and everything about her was so gentle and delicate, that you felt you had to take care of her so that she would not come to any harm.

When he wanted to listen to music, she would put the gramophone on for him, and she was always ready to go around the house with him and look at its contents and tell him about them.

The things were very old, most of them—two or three or even four hundred years old—and the children's father and mother had had them from *their* father and mother, and they in turn had had them from *their* father and mother, and so right back to the time the things were new. And they had always been there in the one place. He could talk for hours with Maria about the people who had lived there long ago—about what they had looked like, what kind of clothes they had worn, what kind of food they had eaten, and what they had thought about.

Sometimes Maria would tell him about going to school, and then David would again be reminded of how different he was, for Maria did not care much about going to school, and David thought it sounded wonderful, more wonderful than anything in the world except sunshine and beauty. To think that there were people whose only work in life was to teach children the things they did not know! To be able to ask about everything you wanted to know without appearing odd and suspicious! It was quite plain that it was not one of *their* schools, since he gathered from Maria that the children were not told what they were to think. They learned proper things—about history and the countries of the world—and they were taught to read quickly and write without making mistakes . . .

David now began to wish he had invented a different story about himself, for his tale of a circus always on the move had led the children and their parents to believe he was familiar with many countries. If he had chosen another story, he would have been able to ask them about other countries, where they lay and what they were like. Now he dared not, and it was difficult to find out what he wanted to know from books.

If only there had been books about those countries that he could have spotted at once from their titles, then he could have read all he needed to know . . .

It was now growing chilly of an evening. It was the time of the vine harvest—time for him to hurry on his way.

One day David decided to pluck up courage and ask Maria. She had seen a map in school, and so she might perhaps remember what he wanted to know. But when it came to the point, his courage failed him. He remembered what it was like when he and the children went to bed. The children kissed their father and mother, and their father and mother kissed them and then patted them on the shoulder and made them laugh and called them "my precious" and "my treasure." The parents were good with the children, and they belonged together, all of them. They were a family. And members of a family told one another things. So even if he asked Maria not to tell anyone what he asked her, she might very well forget and tell her mother or her father all the same.

It was then that he saw the globe. It stood in Andrea's room, inside a cupboard. David did not know at first what it was. He saw a big ball fastened to a rod. He was curious and asked why it was fastened like that.

"It's a globe, of course!" Andrea replied in surprise. "It's the world . . . Look, you can turn it around so that you can see everything . . ."

David's heart began to beat with excitement. Andrea had the whole world drawn on a sphere— and all the countries in it!

But there were no boundaries marked on it: you could only see where the mountains and valleys and rivers were. David felt quite sick with disappointment. But Andrea was always ready to talk whenever David wanted to discuss something. "There's Italy," he said, pointing to a long strip of land jutting out into the sea.

"And there's France," added Maria, pointing in her turn.

When they saw how interested David was, they continued and pointed to Spain and Germany, Austria, Switzerland, and England.

But they went through them so quickly! David wondered if he could possibly remember all they told him and wished he could see how far each country stretched.

"Can you see Denmark?" he asked, praying inwardly as he spoke. "God, God of the green pastures and the still waters, don't let it be a big country so that they're surprised I don't know where it is! Amen!"

It was quite a little patch of land, and David saw it was a long way from Italy. He could never go so far before winter set in, before *they* found him again.

He would have to leave. David lay in his soft warm bed and knew that he must go the next day, or at least within a day or two. The house belonged to the family, and he had no part in it.

They were still all very grateful that he had rescued Maria from the fire. And he was sure they were kind, all except Carlo, that is. But something was sure to happen soon that would make them realize how different he was. The children's mother sometimes looked at him questioningly, and she no longer attempted to caress him. She would touch his hair lightly when they were going to bed, but David knew it was no longer because she wanted to. She did it only out of kindness so that she should not make too much difference between him and her own children. David was not at all clear how he knew this; he just knew it. It was not because he liked anyone to touch him, either. He hated it; it made him feel tense inside. But sometimes when he saw the children and their parents touch one another, he felt a stab of pain and remembered Johannes. Perhaps he had been like everybody else to start with; perhaps it was only when Johannes died that he became different. Johannes used to lay his hand on him, and he had not hated it and shrunk away then—on the contrary, it had given him a warm, comforted feeling.

But Johannes could never return, and so perhaps it was all to the good that he now hated being touched—if only because there was no one to do it.

There was only Maria. David tried not to think about it, but he had to admit the truth of it. Maria sometimes touched him, and he did not hate it. She would take him by the hand when they walked side by side, and her hand was small and soft, not in the least like a boy's. And when Maria held his hand, it was as if they spoke to one another without saying anything—as if they were speaking of pleasant things together. Yet, it always made him a little uneasy, like something important that had escaped his memory . . .

David turned over in bed. There *was* something he had forgotten—what was it? Something about Denmark, something he had been on the point of remembering the first day he was there.

It had something to do with what the man had said about his having to go north till he came to Denmark. Suddenly he knew what it was—milk!

The children's parents were very good to them. They gave them everything they needed and talked a great deal about what would do them good. Every day the children were given milk and things called vitamins. David had been given them, too, while he had been living in the house. *And he had had milk before* . . .

Twice a week, for as long as he could remember, on Tuesdays and Fridays, he had had to go across to the man's quarters, and the man had given him something white to drink. It tasted horrible, but the man told him he *must* drink it or else he would shoot one of the prisoners. He also threatened to shoot a prisoner if David ever told anyone where he went and what he did. Nothing happened except that David drank the horrible white stuff. At the time

David had thought that it showed how stupid *they* were, as well as wicked. It did not make him ill, and he did not die either, and you would have thought the man would have realized it was not poisonous enough; yet he went on giving it to David to drink.

The milk he was given here did not taste unpleasant, and it was whiter, too, but it was the same for all that. And the first time David happened to bite one of the pills that were called vitamins and drank his milk right on top of it, it tasted horrible in just the same way as it used to in the camp.

So the man had given him something that was good for him—something to make him strong and not always ill and weak and emaciated and listless like the other prisoners!

Why? David sat up in bed, wide awake. Why had he forced him to drink something that was good for him? If he had been of some importance as a hostage, then obviously he must not be allowed to die . . . but, in that case, why had he told David to escape? It had all happened as the man had told him . . . There had been the bundle lying beneath the tree, and he had gotten to Salonika, and there had been a ship there . . .

David got up and dressed. He could not sleep; he could not stay inside the house. He must think . . .

But no matter how much he thought, he could

not find an answer. He walked quietly downstairs into the garden so that no one should hear him if the children's parents or any of the servants were still up. But although he stared out into the darkness and thought about the man as hard as he could, he still could not make head or tail of it. The man hated him. David knew all about hate, and if anything were sure, he was sure the man hated him.

An important hostage would have to be kept alive . . . but he must not be allowed to escape, must he? If only he knew more about it. If only he knew something about Denmark. If there were a king in Denmark, then he would *have* to try to get there. There must be some reason why he was told to escape. For one moment he thought he knew what it was. You could not bribe honest people, but bad people would accept bribery; *they* took bribes. Being bribed meant doing something you knew was forbidden just to get something for yourself.

But who would bribe the man to let David escape? He was just David, a boy who had always been a prisoner. Someone he stood hostage for without knowing it? But who could it be? And *if* he had been an important hostage, then the man would never have dared to let him escape. In that country, they were all terrified of one another. Perhaps if the bribe were big enough . . . but if that were the answer, then *they* would be hunting for him, everywhere, and he would have to be on his guard day and night.

It must not be true. David's hands clutched his fast-beating heart. There must be a reason he could not understand; he did not want to be an important hostage, for he could not go on being as frightened as he was. The next morning he would ask the children's father if there were a king in Denmark. And if so, then he would have to take his leave at once, and he would have to travel by car as often as possible or he would not manage the journey. But it would not do for him to believe he was an important hostage, for if he did, he would not dare ask for a lift or earn money or buy bread or anything.

David felt as if the surrounding darkness were entering into him, penetrating deeply into all his thoughts until he was unable to recall one faint gleam of hope. He was aware only of fear, of the need to be constantly on his guard.

But he never got as far as asking the children's father if there were a king in Denmark.

He decided he would creep back to bed again, but just as he was going past the big living room that opened onto the terrace, the light was switched on and the children's father and mother entered and sat down.

David pressed himself against the wall and stood still. When they began talking, he would creep off in the other direction so they would not spot him.

Through the slats in the shutters he saw the children's mother take up her sewing. She put it down again almost at once and, turning to her husband, said, "Giovanni, I think you'll have to do something about David."

David moved with infinite care away from the slatted shutters; sometimes when you were looking at people, they became aware of it. He leaned against the wall and shut his eyes. Suppose he had fallen asleep and they had surprised him there the next day!

"What should I do about him, Elsa? Is there something the matter with him?"

David would never forget what they said; he would remember every word as long as he lived.

"The matter . . . ? Yes, I . . . I mean, how long do you suppose he should stay here?"

"Have you anything against the lad, my dear?"

"Yes . . . no . . . Oh, you must understand I'm bound to love a child that's saved my own child's life. But I don't understand him . . . If it didn't sound so absurd, I'd be inclined to say he frightens me."

"He's an unusual child, that I grant you. But I can't see what you have against him."

"I . . . well, let me put it this way. I've nothing against David as David, but I do object to him as company for my own children. He must leave here as soon as possible."

"Can't you tell me exactly what it is about him that you object to?"

"I don't know who he is. I don't know where he comes from, and I don't know where he's going to. I don't believe he's truthful. That story of his about belonging to a circus—it doesn't hang together properly. Giovanni! If he belongs to a circus, there are things he ought to know that he obviously doesn't. And at the same time, the story's so carefully worked out—as if he were a hardened little liar . . ."

"With eyes like his, Elsa?"

"Yes . . . And his eyes frighten me, too. They're the eyes of an old man, an old man who's seen so much in life that he no longer cares to go on living. They're not even desperate . . . just quiet and expectant and very, very lonely, as if he were quite alone of his own free choice . . . Giovanni, a child's eyes don't look like that! There's something wrong there . . . And his smile . . . if it weren't so incredible, I'd be tempted to say he looks as if he'd never smiled before he set eyes on Maria. He never smiles at the rest of us: he just looks at us politely and with dead earnestness, and when he smiles at Maria, it's . . ."

"It's very beautiful, Elsa. I've seen it myself. It comes so hesitantly and yet so tenderly . . ."

"Oh, you make me feel so heartless! But I must put my own children first and think of their welfare. And there's something wrong with a child who smiles like that. Where does he come from? You can tell he has no near relatives, but he makes it quite clear he doesn't like us to question him. He answers politely, but his face becomes watchful and he replies as briefly as he can. It's not that I want to pry, Giovanni, but you must admit he's a strange child! He arrives here out of the blue, dressed in a pair of trousers and a shirt both in such a shocking condition that even the poorest beggar is better off. He owns a knife and an empty bottle, which he obviously regards as vital necessities. And yet he speaks Italian like a Florentine nobleman!"

"Yes, and French like a senior member of the French Academy!"

"*What* does he do?"

"I found him with a French book the other day, and he asked me to read a few lines to him. I naturally thought he wanted them translated, but he explained it wasn't necessary; he only wanted to compare the sound of the words with their appearance in print! He's obviously never seen French written, but I can assure you he speaks it like a native! And like a very gifted and well-educated native, too!"

"Yes, and then I suppose he explained it away by saying, 'There was a man in the circus who was French'?"

"Exactly. Heaven knows what kind of circus it is!"

"I'm quite sure there is no circus. Can't you see there's something mysterious and wrong about it all? At first I imagined he'd run away from school or something of the sort, but to judge from his speech, you'd think he came from a family that would have moved heaven and earth long enough ago to find him, and yet there's not been a word about a search being made for a child of any of the people we know. So where does he get his speech from? And when you consider it, he doesn't speak like a child at all. His conversation is completely adult, and he often fails to understand what the children mean until they explain to him . . . He really makes you think he'd never before spoken to another child!"

"That can hardly be the case. But wherever he comes from, Elsa, we are deeply indebted to him, and since it worries him to be questioned about his background, then I think we ought to let him alone. I can't see either that any of the things you've mentioned can be said to make him unsuitable company for our children. He talks beautifully, and he has really charming manners—often better than our own youngsters'—that seem to come from a quite instinctive knowledge that consideration and respect for other people's rights are the only way to live peacefully and satisfactorily together. Elsa, Elsa, why don't you use your eyes? I admit he's a strange child, and I admit there's something mysterious about him, but I can't imagine he could be a bad influence . . . David's the gentlest boy I've ever seen in my life! And he's had an effect on our own children—I haven't once seen them fighting since he came!"

"No, and it's on the tip of my tongue to say I wish they did! You ask me what I have against David: I object to his attitude to Carlo, and I object to his relations with Maria. Haven't you seen that David hates Carlo? Not like boys who fight and then forget about it because there was really nothing serious to fight over. David hates Carlo as a grown man hates. He talks to him only when he has to, and then he speaks politely and coldly and refuses to look at him. Try watching Carlo a little more closely tomorrow! He's grown quite subdued, and when he sees David and Andrea chattering together, he just stands there looking rather wistful, but he doesn't join in. He seems to know that if he did, David would immediately bring the conversation to a polite close and go off elsewhere. Carlo's a good boy. He's a little wild and somewhat domineering over the others, but otherwise there's no harm in him. Do you suppose it gives me any pleasure to see my eldest son trying to ingratiate himself with a lying little vagabond and being rebuffed with hatred and contempt?"

"No, of course not . . . but don't you think you might be mistaken? Suppose we asked David . . ."

"And I like his influence over Maria just as little. Maria worships the ground he treads on. Everything David thinks and says and does is right. She is aware of the existence of her own brothers only when it suits David. What she likes best is being alone with David—the other day she sat quite still for a whole hour listening to the gramophone with him: Mozart's violin concerto! What do you make of that? And Maria's about as musical as a sucking pig!"

"Well, yes . . . but it can't do any harm, my dear. Little girls often admire boys a little bigger than themselves . . . And you must remember that it was David who rescued her from the fire. It's quite natural for her to admire him. She used to admire Carlo and Andrea as well."

"But not in the same way. She admired the two bigger boys because they were stronger and more daring. With David it's himself that she admires . . . and it isn't just admiration either—it's devotion! She seems to want to know and understand everything he thinks so that she can learn to think the same way herself. Giovanni, I won't have it! I've listened to the two of them together when they didn't know I was there . . . With the rest of us David is silent and reticent, but he talks to Maria because it never occurs to her to question him, except to ask him what he thinks about things. He tells her the most abominable things . . . about wickedness and misery and brutality . . . and treachery. And he's told her how you die so that it doesn't hurt . . . I don't know where he gets it all from, and I don't care either. That boy must go!"

"I would never have thought David had a brutal mind or an inclination to cruelty . . ."

"He hasn't. He tells her about such things so that she can take care of herself and so that she may know how fortunate she is. But I will not have my children listening to things of that nature. They've time enough to learn that there's wickedness in the world. I'll not have my son trying in vain to win the good graces of a lying little stranger whom we know nothing about, and I'll not have Maria's sweet child-like, carefree attitude to life spoiled by a knowledge of evil she had no idea of. Children have their own troubles . . . they mustn't be expected to bear the miseries and sorrows of the grown-up world."

"Well, since you feel so strongly about it, then . . . But don't you think that if perhaps I spoke to the boy about it . . . ?"

"Do you think that anything at all that anyone could say to David would alter by one jot what he thinks? Do you think anybody in the world could stop David being David?"

"No, my dear, I don't think they could, and I must say I respect him for it. The lad isn't obstinate or headstrong, and he wants to learn, but he reserves the right to think for himself, and he'll not surrender his personality. And that's good: it shows strength of character."

"Giovanni . . . I'm not heartless. I really am grateful, and I'll willingly do anything for the boy but keep him here. I don't believe there's any real harm in him, and I can see that a great deal of what you say about him is right, and if he weren't a child, I should most probably like him for those very things. But I don't understand him . . . and I won't have him influencing my own children. Can't you find out something about him? Try to tell him we wish him well and see if you can discover where he comes from? If he's done something wrong, then you could use your influence with the police . . . We could send him to a home or a monastery or something of the sort and pay for his education . . . but he'll have to tell you the truth so that we can decide the best thing to do . . ."

"All right, Elsa, as you wish."

"You're not to count the cost—that doesn't matter. He's to have the best of everything—clothes, food, education—for Maria's sake . . . and because I could have loved him so much if he had been willing to let me . . ."

David sat down on the windowsill and stared into the darkness. Every word the children's parents had said to one another was deeply engraved upon his mind. His hands, his legs, his whole body were shaking, and he was unable to control himself. He had realized that he must go and go soon, but the fact that danger was so near at hand was something he had not realized. And now he had been made aware of all that was amiss with him . . . and he knew he could never put it right. He did not really think he was so amiss, but other people obviously thought so.

In the morning the children's father would try to question him, and when he found he was getting nowhere, he would call in the police . . . in the belief that he could still take care of David even after *they* had laid hands on him.

He must leave that very night.

David took his bundle out of the cupboard, together with his bottle, his knife, and his small scrap of soap. For one moment he considered taking a larger piece of soap from the bathroom. He would like to have taken a sponge and his toothbrush as well, and a candle and some fresh matches. But then he decided not to. He would have to go in Andrea's clothes, which he was wearing, for the children's mother had never given him back his own and she had said he might have them. But apart from the clothes that he had to keep on, he would take nothing at all with him, although she and the children's father had talked of all they were willing to give him.

They were not wicked people. They had been kind to him, and even though they were ready to give him up now, they were acting out of ignorance, since they had no idea what would happen when *they* caught him again. He would have to be gone from the house before they arrived the next day, but he would write a letter so that he could at least say thank you. He had the paper and pencil he had bought. It would take a long time, and he would have to hurry so that he could be well on his way before morning . . . but that he could not help.

David sat down and thought for a long time. Then he wrote very, very slowly and very carefully.

"I heard everything you said. I shall go now, as soon as I've finished writing. I only wanted to stay here as long as you wished me to. I shall have to keep Andrea's clothes because you have not given me my own. I want to thank you for letting me listen to music and read books, and because everything is so beautiful here. And thank you for the food you have given me and for letting me sleep in a bed.

"I want to tell you quite freely that I have never murdered anyone and never used force. And I've never stolen from anybody; I've taken no one's joy or happiness or freedom or property away from him. And I've never betrayed anyone; nothing dreadful has ever happened, because I have never been a traitor. I am telling you this because you want to know something about me and to let you know that that's all I am going to tell. If the police catch me,

I shall die, but I shall tell them nothing more than that. It is important not to give in to people who love violence and think they have the right to take away another person's life and liberty. And if you don't let them change what you think and believe, then you have won. A man once told me that. And that's why I'm going to stay as I am, always, as long as I live.

"I am glad I told Maria that wickedness exists. I don't want her to be afraid, but it's something you have to know about. Can't you understand that children have a right to know everything that's true? If there's danger, you have to recognize it, or else you can't take care of yourself. I mean other children, those that aren't wrong and have somewhere to belong to.

"I am writing because I want to say thank you for the things you have given me and to tell you of my own free will all that I'm going to tell.

"David."

It had taken him a frightfully long time. David looked at the clock on the chest of drawers—it was now half-past one in the morning. He wanted to write something about Maria, something that would make them take great care of her . . . but he could not do it. He thought of so many things in connection with her; he could not bear the thought of having to go away.

Suddenly, as if she had overheard his thoughts, she was standing there in the doorway. She was in her white nightdress, her hair loose . . . looking frightened.

"David . . ."

"Sh!" David whispered in alarm. Maria came into the room, shutting the door behind her.

"David . . . I woke up so frightened. I thought you were in the fire and I couldn't find you . . ."

"I've got to go away, Maria," David said.

"Oh, no, David! . . . Why?"

David told her everything her parents had said while he was standing outside within earshot. "So you see I must go now while it's still night," he concluded when she had heard everything.

Fortunately, Maria never doubted that what he said was right. She made no protest; she just looked at him earnestly and said quite quietly, "David . . . you'll come back, won't you? Even if it's not for a long time . . . say you'll come back . . ."

David looked at her dumbly. How could he say that? The children's mother had called him a liar. But this was something quite different. People didn't understand that your life depended on having a good story, one that *they* couldn't prove wrong, and on never allowing yourself to be shaken from it. But this was different. Maria didn't belong to *them*, and what she was asking was a promise. Johannes had told him promises were important. A man must respect his own promises if he wanted others to respect *him*.

Then he said, "I can't say that. If I can, in time, come, then I will . . . but I don't know, and so I won't promise."

"But, David, who's going to tell me about everything when you're gone?"

Ah, yes, who would look after Maria . . . ? How could he when he had to leave her? And if he did not go, *they* would come and take him, and so he would not be able to look after her anyway. Then David did something he had never done before: of his own free will he touched somebody else. He laid his hands on Maria's shoulders and looked straight into her eyes. Then he said slowly so that she could remember what he said and try to understand it:

"You must do it yourself, Maria! You must teach yourself all about things and look after yourself. When there's no one else to do things for you, you have to do them for yourself. You must listen carefully to the people you think are good—your father and mother and the people that teach you things in school. Then you must think over what they say and decide how much of it you feel is right. But you must be careful, because what is right is not always what you want, and if you make a mistake, you regret it afterward . . ."

"But, David, I'm not clever enough . . . Oh, why do you have to go when I'd much rather you stayed? Will you take me with you?"

"I'd like to, but it wouldn't be right. Your father and mother would be frightened, and you've no right to make anyone afraid. In a way, it's like using violence. And you wouldn't have a very good time, either; I've often no food and nowhere to sleep . . ."

"That wouldn't matter if you were there . . . But since you say it's wrong, then you shan't take me with you . . ."

"You can think about me, Maria, and then I shan't be quite gone . . ."

"Will you think about me, too?"

"Yes."

"Always?"

"Yes."

David put his comb, pencil, and paper in his bundle. He had everything now. Meanwhile, Maria stood watching him. Then she said, "David, wait here a moment . . ."

David stood and waited quite calmly; Maria would

never give him away. A moment later she was back, holding in her hand a little cross of gold, covered with tiny little seed pearls. "That's for you, David, to take with you."

The cross hung on a slender chain, and she stood on tiptoe to fasten it around David's neck.

"Thank you," David said. "Now I'm going." He put his bundle on the table, and she flung her arms around his neck. She was soft and warm, just as she had been the day he had rescued her from the fire.

"We'll be able to remember now," she whispered.

"Yes," David replied, and for a moment they looked into one another's eyes . . . Maria's black eyes and sweet face that had taught him how to smile . . . David took her face in both his hands and kissed her.

"Good-bye, Maria."

"Good-bye, David."

David went quickly and, without looking at her again, shut the door softly behind him.

6

David tramped on and on. He was so familiar with the first part of the way that the darkness did not trouble him—he had often been along that road with the children. He told himself he would take his shoes off as soon as it was morning, for he had noticed while he was in the house that shoes wore out, and it would be a good thing to save the shoes for later on when it grew colder or he was forced to travel at night when he could not see the stones.

He thought, too, about the route he had to take. He would have to go into a town called Florence, for of course he had no food. Luckily he still had a lot of money given to him by the American he had fetched petrol for . . . so he had no need to stop in the town to earn more. But thinking about food for any length of time made him feel uneasy, for then he found himself thinking about milk and vitamins, and from there he would go on to wonder whether he might perhaps be an important hostage.

But he had learned a lot from his stay in the house. The globe . . . he must remember to think about the globe all the time so that he would not forget where Andrea and Maria had pointed. He must get to Switzerland first . . . and then he would come to Germany and finally to Denmark. His clothes were a great help, too—they were much better than the ones he had had before, and there were more of them. They would help a lot now that it was growing cold during the nights.

Yet his thoughts remained heavy and depressed in spite of his recalling all the added advantages he had gained from living in the house.

And as the days went by, he felt no better, although all the places he came to were just as beautiful as those he had passed through before he came to the house. There were beautiful round green hills, and valleys and rivers, and trees of all kinds. Everything looked the same as before and yet seemed different.

For the first few days he dared not risk traveling by car; he would not try asking for a lift until he was a long way from the house. He made haste to leave Florence, too, although there were so many things to see there—a great river with a great bridge over it, and on the bridge a narrow street complete with old houses on either side. And there was a square with big statues in it, and a church that looked like . . . David could find nothing to compare it with, it was so beautiful. While he had been living in the house, he had heard that there were places in Florence where there were thousands of magnificent paintings that everybody could see . . . and he would like to have gone to look at them. But the great thing was to get far away from the house as quickly as he could. The farther away he went, the more difficult would it be for *them* to discover which way he was going.

So far no one had questioned him. As long as he had money to buy bread, he had no need to talk to the tourists, and they were the ones who always asked the most questions. The Italians only wanted to know what he was called and where he was going. David was very careful what he said about the circus now. If only he could find out where he had shown his ignorance, as the children's mother had said he had. In spite of everything, he still thought it was the best story he could find.

He thought often of what the children's parents had said about him. He was a little upset by it, but not very much, for he had known all along that he was not like other boys and that there was something about him that people found strange. But he did not think the children's mother had explained very clearly just where he was different. His manner of speech, for instance. He had, of course, heard many Italians speak somewhat differently . . . but then the children's parents spoke just as he did! Just like the Italian priest in the concentration camp. And the French he spoke was certainly good French, for that was Johannes' own language, the language David was so familiar with that the French word would often occur to him before he could remember the Italian. And as Johannes, who was wiser and better than anybody else, spoke French in that way, then it must be the proper way.

Perhaps that was the trouble . . . perhaps you *shouldn't* speak well if you were a tramp? But if that was what the children's mother had meant, then she was wrong. The way you spoke was a reflection of how you thought, and that could not possibly have anything to do with whether you were a tramp or whether you had somewhere to live and had many things of your own.

And as for hating Carlo, yes, it was true enough, he did. And when he thought about it, he could well understand the children's mother not liking it, for, of course, she did not know Carlo was bad. But there was nothing to be done about it; he could not have stopped hating Carlo, not even if Maria herself had begged him to. You must always hate what was bad or else you grew just like *them*.

No, there was nothing he could do to put matters right except by making a complete change in himself, and that he would not do—he must always be true to himself.

He would beg a lift the next day so that he could get quickly to the town called Bologna, for since leaving Florence, the mountains had become quite high and it was taking him longer to go uphill.

David began to think about Switzerland. There he would find lofty mountains without trees, capped with eternal snow. That much he understood from Andrea when they had looked at the globe together.

But he seemed unable to direct his thoughts properly; they were full of heaviness and foreboding, so that nothing felt right. Just before the bend in the road he had noticed a small town not far ahead, and he now decided he would try to pluck up enough courage to go into the church.

The houses had a friendly look about them, and the hour was about noon, when there was hardly anyone in the streets. David remained standing in the open space that was always to be found in front of a church and wondered if he dared.

His mood of depression was the result of his having entered a house, but a church was not a house, of course—no one lived there. And he had wanted for such a long time to see what a church was like . . . A church was a place where you talked with God. In Italy, of course, he would only find the God of the Roman Catholics, but still—suppose his own God were on a visit there! And suppose he really met Him! But perhaps gods did not visit one another . . . A faint hope that he would find some comfort there drove him inside.

The door was heavy. Even in small towns like this one, the church was always big and the door was just as heavy as the front door of the house where he had been staying. He had to push hard to open it.

The light inside was subdued. David remained standing just inside the door until his eyes had grown accustomed to the change from the bright sunlight outside to the soft obscurity within.

It was very quiet—and beautiful. It reminded him a little of the house, though in many ways it was very different. There were paintings and carved woodwork and colored glass in the windows. In front of some of the paintings along the side of the church, candles were burning.

But the silence was not complete. David's eyes,

now accustomed to the dim light, perceived a dark figure kneeling before one of the paintings. The man was saying something, very softly.

David crept quietly toward him. If it were someone praying, he wanted to listen. He might learn something. But he could not understand the words . . . It was . . . yes, it was Latin, and apart from a few words, he knew no Latin.

The figure rose. "Good day, my son. Are you looking for something?"

"No, sir," David replied politely. He stepped back hastily and glanced over his shoulder to make sure where the door lay.

"You need not be frightened of me . . . As you can see, I'm a priest . . ."

David realized he was right. Priests always wore long black gowns—outside the concentration camp. And a priest was never one of *them*. David ceased looking toward the door and looked at the painting instead.

"Is that your God, sir?"

"No, that's Saint Christopher."

"He's not a god?"

"There's only one God, my son."

David frowned . . . That wasn't right; he *knew* there were several.

"What are you called, my son?"

"I am David."

"So you're David . . . and who's your God, David?"

"He's the God of the green pastures and the still waters . . ."

The priest looked at him and smiled. " 'The Lord is my shepherd; I shall not want. He maketh me to lie down in green pastures: He leadeth me beside the still waters. He restoreth my soul: He leadeth me in the paths of righteousness for His Name's sake. Yea, though I walk through the valley of the shadow of death, I will fear no evil, for Thou art with me . . .' It's the same God, David."

David had listened attentively . . . He loved the sound of the strange words that people did not otherwise use, and the priest seemed quite familiar with his God.

"It can't be the same one, signor . . . He was the God of someone who was also called David."

"Yes, that's right. The words I spoke come from the twenty-third psalm of David. I gather you must be a stranger and don't belong to our church. But, believe me, David, it's the same God . . . We men call Him by so many different names, but when we pray because we need help or comfort, it's still the same God that hears our prayers."

Perhaps what the priest said was true. How could

he be sure, when there were so many things he did not know? But when you had made a choice, then you must stand by it, even if your choice concerned God, and if the priest were mistaken, you mustn't let yourself be influenced by it . . .

"I'd rather keep my own God, if you don't mind, signor. He's very strong and helps you when you're frightened. And you shouldn't change your mind once you've made your choice, for you must respect what you've said . . ."

David said this very politely, for he did not want to hurt the priest's feelings.

But the priest did not seem to mind in the least. He continued to smile and said in a voice so gentle that it sounded almost like Johannes', "You are perfectly right, David, and you've chosen well. You shall certainly not want. Do you know what 'want' means?"

"Yes, it's the same as being in need . . . but I like the other word better. It sounds more—more like music."

David no longer felt sure it was quite so simple as that. People were often in need, but they had to do something about it themselves; they could not get something for nothing.

David thought the priest was going to put his hand out toward him, and he stiffened. But he was wrong; the priest did not touch him but merely said, "I'm going home for something to eat, David. If you're hungry, you can come with me. Or perhaps I can help you in some other way?"

David considered. A priest was never dangerous, and it would be foolish not to accept help in finding out what he wanted to know. "Thank you," he said. "I'm not hungry, but if you have a map that shows what Italy looks like, then I'd like to see where Switzerland begins."

Beyond Bologna the countryside was less beautiful. The landscape was practically flat and the road gray and dusty. Some of the byroads might have been more picturesque, as David had discovered they often were, but he was in a hurry, and there was more traffic on the main roads. He had written down on a piece of paper the names of the towns he must pass through on his way to Switzerland, and as it was growing a little bit colder every night, David only stopped when he ran short of bread. He had now spent all the money he had started with, and it was only in the towns that he could earn more. But there were no longer so many tourists to be found, and David wondered if they would all go back home when the weather became really cold. If they did, he would be in danger of starving, for the Italians were able to do most things for themselves and did not need a boy to help them. Moreover, although he was by this time a very long way from the house, the thought never left him that they might have put the police onto him, and so he considered it safer to keep away from Italians, except for motorists and truck drivers.

They were quite safe. They had no time to be interested in strange boys; they were too fully occupied with thinking where they were going and what they were going to do when they got back home. As long as you listened to what they told you about themselves and their families, they were satisfied. They always said how nice it was to have someone to talk with, but David thought they really meant "talk to" rather than "talk with," for there was never any need for him to say much more than "yes" or "no." But that suited him. As long as they were only interested in themselves, there was less danger of their asking him too many questions. And they nearly always shared their food with him.

Then there was the driver who had introduced David to railway stations. He had very often seen trains, but it had never occurred to him that they had definite stopping places or that there were such things as stations. That was before he got to Milan. The man he had been riding with had asked him something or other about the circus, and David had told him he had been taken ill when they were in Naples and so he was now alone on the roads on his way to join the circus again. The man inquired if he had enough money, and when David replied that he occasionally earned a little, the man apparently thought he was in the habit of doing it at railway stations.

So when he arrived in Milan, David went in search of the station. And what a good way of earning money it was! The people who were boarding the trains or getting off them were often in need of someone to carry their cases, and at the station there were still many tourists to be found who did not know Italian and were glad of someone who understood what they said and could find out what they wanted to know, like asking which platforms the trains were due to go from or where the restaurant was. David spent a whole evening at the station and earned enough money to buy bread for several days.

It was there he saw the paper.

He was no longer so interested in newspapers. Whenever he came across one or had the loaf he bought wrapped in one, he would read what was in it to practice reading quickly, but much of it was about things he knew nothing of, and in any case he had no means of knowing how much of what he read was true, especially when he did not know who had written the articles. If *they* had written them, then it was best not to believe them.

Suddenly he saw his own name!

He had been sitting on a seat for a little rest, for the last case he had carried had been very heavy and he was tired. An Italian was sitting beside him, and when he got up to go, he left his paper lying on the seat.

And there on the back page he read: "David. Do not be afraid. We are not searching for you. But we should be glad if you would come back and live with us. We believe everything you said. The children's parents."

It was addressed to him—there was no doubt about that—and for a little while he felt quite happy . . .

It was cold in the ditch. He dared not try to beg a lift in the evening because people thought it wrong for a boy to be on the roads at that time. It had taken him a long while to leave Milan behind, and now he could find nowhere to sleep but this ditch. It was a good thing he had grown used to being cold in the camp. Once more David thought about the letter in the paper. He was glad they had written to him. They were good people, all of them—all except Carlo.

Yet he knew he could not go back. He would always hate Carlo, and he would always be different and out of place. And he would not be able to tell them what they wanted to know, for if he did, they would be forced to send him back to *them*.

Suddenly David knew why nothing had seemed quite right since he had left the house. He recalled how uneasy he had felt as he had gone up the broad front steps the first day he was there—as if some danger lay in wait for him behind those doors. If only he had gone on his way and never entered the place! He had been happy before . . . yes, happy. When he had lived among the rocks and while he was tramping the roads, he had been his own master and could do as he pleased. He had had the beauty of the countryside all about him, he had enjoyed the taste of bread and fruit, and he could wash whenever he wanted and go where he would. But when he entered the house, his old way of life lost some of its value.

He had seen what he could never have, and nothing would ever again appear quite so good and satisfying as it had done before he had learned of the existence of that other life. Even if he had not hated Carlo, even if he had dared to go back, it would not have helped matters. The children and their parents belonged to one another, and David could never belong. He was not . . . *right*. He was different from other children who had not been brought up in a concentration camp. There was nowhere he belonged. Now that they no longer believed he was really bad, they would do their utmost to make it appear that he did belong, but it would not be the truth. He would continue to be himself, David, a boy who had been a fugitive and did not know where he was fleeing to.

He should never have entered the house. Maria . . . whenever he had looked at Maria and she had brought a smile to his lips, he had been aware that there was something he had forgotten, something important.

He had forgotten the most important condition that made it possible for him to go on living, that he should never again grow fond of anyone. When Johannes died, he thought he would die, too. But when he had recovered and knew he was not going to die, he realized he must never, never care for anyone again—never. Only if you were indifferent could you go on living. And that was what he had kept in mind through all the years that followed. But when he saw Maria, it was forgotten.

And now nothing would ever be as it was before. Even if they were not looking for him, even if he could preserve his liberty and could avoid being too cold or too hungry, it would never be the same again: another boy had appeared, one who was not different from the rest, one who felt he belonged to a place and to people, one who was loved by someone he could love in return. And yet he would always have to remain himself.

"God," he said. "God of the green pastures and the still waters. I'm not praying for help, because I am David and that's something that can't be altered. But I want You to know that I've found out that green pastures and still waters are not enough to live by . . . nor is freedom. Not when you know there's love and you haven't anyone you belong to because you're different and are only a boy who's run away. I'm saying this to tell You You needn't help me anymore to escape from *them*. It doesn't matter. Thank You for the times You helped me when I still thought life might be a little worth living. I am David. Amen."

David could not remember when he had stopped crying. He had not cried since Johannes died, only that first day in Italy and the day among the rocks, and that was only water running from his eyes, not from sorrow or sadness as it is when you cry properly. He must have fallen asleep in the end, for when he looked about him again, it was morning and the sun was shining. It must have been shining for some time, for he was no longer perished with cold as he had been during the night.

He felt completely tired; a feeling of exhaustion seemed to go right through him. He got up, picked up his bundle, and started to walk. He might just as well walk as sit there and wait.

He thought of nothing in particular. There was no longer any need to think, now that he did not care what happened.

He took it into his head, however, to find his way around the frontier post. He did not know why he was doing it. What they called instinct, perhaps, or the urge for self-preservation—whatever it was that made men strive to go on living, even when they knew it would be better to die. Or perhaps it was because the scenery had become beautiful again. When he had reached a place called Como, he had found the mountains once more. The town lay on the shores of a large blue lake surrounded by magnificent mountains, and people were laughing gaily in the streets.

The frontier lay in the next village, and David knew at once he was not going to like it. There was a barrier across the road and soldiers who examined people's passports before they were allowed to drive on. It all looked very friendly, and no one seemed to be afraid. They all had their papers in order, of course, and so they were allowed to proceed. But David did not like the look of it. If he had to be arrested, then it would be in the beauty of the mountains, not here at a road barrier. He made his way out of the village again and along a narrow byroad, and not until he had been walking for an hour did he turn northward, away from the road. He had learned in the concentration camp that this was the way to cross a frontier, at some point where no one could see you. Sometimes you were caught in spite of that, but then it was by chance and not because there was a barrier there.

For a long time he tramped on, away from the road, up over the vineyards, keeping as nearly in a northerly direction as he could reckon from the position of the sun. It was hard going, but he wanted to be quite sure he had crossed the frontier before he took to the roads again. Then he came to a village called Mendrisio and immediately concluded he had gone astray, for the people in the street still spoke Italian. But then he saw a notice over a doorway with the word *Svizzero* on it and a flag that was not the Italian flag. *Svizzero*, he recalled, was the Italian word for Switzerland. So they spoke Italian in Switzerland, too.

David decided to take the road again; it was only the barrier that he wanted to avoid. He knew nothing about Switzerland, not a thing . . . There had never been a Swiss in the camp; pure luck, perhaps . . . not that it mattered now.

Late in the afternoon he came to the lake again . . . or it might have been another lake. It was very beautiful, almost as beautiful as the coast where he had lived among the rocks. Dotted up and down the mountainsides lay gay little villages, and boats were sailing on the lake. After he had walked along the shore of the lake for some time, the road ran over a bridge to the other side of the water. The next town should be called Lugano; he would buy a loaf there, and perhaps some cheese as well.

But David did not reach Lugano. The road lay between the mountains and the edge of the lake, and a little above the road he caught sight of an orange tree. He began to scramble up the hillside to see if there were any fallen oranges. He found one and stood there gazing down at the lake, which looked very beautiful from up there. He made his way among the trees still farther up the slope, and there he sat down on a low wall that had been warmed by the sun. He took out his knife and began peeling the orange, gazing now and then at the lake below.

"Hello, boy!"

David turned around to look. He did so quite calmly, for he did not mind who came now. Then he stood up. It was a woman. The children's father always stood up when their mother entered the room, and he made the boys stand up, too.

"I'd like you to let me paint you, if you've time . . ."

David looked at her. "I've plenty of time," he said politely. "But I don't know what it's like to be painted. Where do you want to paint?"

The woman had begun putting something up on an easel—a case was standing at her side. "Here," she said.

David walked over to her and looked at the easel. "Oh, I didn't know you wanted to paint a picture . . . Can you paint beautiful pictures, signora?"

The woman laughed. "No, they're terrible! But just trying is something, isn't it? You always go on hoping that one day you'll manage it."

"Yes. But one day you may realize you'll never be able to."

The woman looked at him as if she were going to say something, but David felt sure that what she did say was not what she was going to say. She merely asked if he could sit still.

David said yes, and she laughed and said she was sure that was a lie, but a quarter of an hour later she begged his pardon; he obviously *could* sit still. But he could move his head and talk now if he wanted to, as long as he kept the rest of his body still.

David answered politely that he had nothing to talk about, and the woman did not appear to find anything odd about that. She went on painting and left David to watch her at his leisure.

She was not a young woman, but she was not old, either. She was thin, and David did not really know whether he liked the look of her. She was not Italian, for she did not speak the language properly; she could say anything she wanted to, but she did not always know which words took masculine endings and which feminine. Her hair was quite fair, and her eyes were gray. She was not pretty or good looking, and yet there was nothing about her face that was unpleasant. And she was intelligent; you could always tell from people's faces whether they were intelligent or not.

David decided that he could find nothing against her. She did not think it necessary to question or talk to him, and when she said anything, she spoke properly, not in the silly manner some people adopted when they were speaking to children, as if you were bound to be stupid just because you were a child.

Several hours went by. The sun sank lower and lower, and the shadows grew longer. Suddenly the woman said, "You're a fool, boy. Why didn't you say it was late? You must be dead beat with all this sitting still!"

"No, I don't mind," David replied.

"Well, if you're hungry, you'd better help me pack up, and then we can go home and get something to eat."

She lived in a beautiful house . . . It was not very big, but it shone with a fresh coat of yellow color-wash. It had green shutters and little balconies outside the windows, and there was a garden all around it with cypresses and palm trees. The inside of the house was very attractive, too. Pictures and other interesting things hung on the whitewashed walls, and the furniture was very fine and quite different from anything David had ever seen before.

The woman said he could set the table while she prepared a meal for them—if he could manage it, that is. But he was not to break anything.

It was fun. The children had often said something was fun, and David had never quite understood what they meant. But being left alone in a beautiful room to find the right things to put on the table and setting them out to his liking—that was certainly fun.

"Heaven preserve us!" exclaimed the woman as she came in. David had not been able to find a white cloth, nor were there any silver plates to put under the ones you ate from. But he had discovered a piece of cloth the color of the mountains where he had lived by the sea—something between red and brown. The woman had attractive plates, and her knives and forks were silver. She had beautiful fine glassware, too, tucked away at the back of a cupboard, and David had placed one of the two candlesticks from the chest of drawers at one end of the table. And there was a black bowl, beautifully shaped, which David had set beside the candlestick. He had picked a pink flower from outside the window and laid it in the bowl.

"Where did you learn to set a table, young man?"

David looked at her. "I like it to look pretty— I mean beautiful, when I eat," he said seriously.

"I beg your pardon. I'd no intention of being nosy, and you're perfectly right: what one does every day should be done beautifully. It's very sensible and proper."

Yes, she was a clever woman. She had noticed that he had not given her a direct answer.

David was gradually growing to like her better and better. They talked of many things while they ate, food and furniture and colors, and she never once seemed surprised by anything he said. She spoke to him as if he were a person who understood what she was saying. David decided to ask her all the things he wanted to know. He would not tell her where he came from; he would just ask questions. It no longer mattered if he aroused suspicion . . . and it would be a good thing to risk asking questions, just for once, without wondering if he were giving himself away.

But no matter what David asked about, she told him what he wanted to know without asking him anything in return. Finally David said, "Is there a king in Denmark?"

"Yes, there is. I must see if I can find a picture of him. How did you know I was Danish? Of course, you probably live down in the village . . ."

"No. I didn't know you were. I only wanted to know whether there was a king."

"Well, I am Danish, anyway. My name's Sophie Hartmann."

"I am called David."

The woman had not asked him, but he thought it was only right that she should know who he was when she had told him who she was herself.

"David?" said the woman. "One rarely hears that name outside England."

"Do you think it's an English name?"

"No, it comes from the Bible . . . most names do originally. It's found in many places, but I've only known one person of that name myself—and I never actually saw him . . ."

David looked at her with interest and waited for her to tell him more, but she said hastily, "There's no reason why I should tell you about that; it was a very sad story, a story of great wickedness."

So they spoke of other things. She showed him a magazine with a big picture on the front cover, a photograph of the king and queen of Denmark. David examined it closely. The king was wearing a uniform with epaulets on his shoulders and many orders on his breast, and the queen looked like a woman in a painting dressed in a long sleeveless gown that revealed her beautiful arms. On her head she wore a large piece of jewelry.

"Well, do you think it's a good photograph?" asked Signora Hartmann.

"I don't know what a king and queen ought to look like," David replied. "But they don't look like people who would break their promises or think they had a right to take other people's lives or freedom away from them. So they must be all right . . . Thank you for showing them to me."

David lay in a bed again that night. Signora Hartmann had told him he could stay overnight if he had nothing else to do and then spend the next day with her. David had told his tale of the circus. He did not like telling it, but what else was he to say? And he had to say something when she asked if he was expected anywhere.

It had been interesting to talk with her. If it had happened before he had decided life could never be worth living, his meeting with her would have given him a lot of pleasure and satisfaction. He was beyond caring now. But she had beautiful things around her, and it was beautiful by the lake, so he might as well spend the day there. She had to go to Rome the next day, she had told him.

David found it difficult to go to sleep. He was not quite so miserable any longer. After all, he had always known it did not matter whether you died or not; it was only after he had made his escape that he had come to think he really did want to live. But he could not get back to his old habits; he went on turning things over in his mind. He could no longer think of nothing as he had trained himself to do in the concentration camp.

When he awoke the next morning, he could hear the signora talking to someone, and he decided to stay in bed until she was alone again. They were speaking in French, and the other person was a man who wanted her to go out sailing with him. She told him she could not because she had a visitor, a boy she was painting. The man asked if it was one of the youngsters from the village, and the signora said no, he belonged to a circus. But she did not add, as David expected, that he "was a strange boy." She said, "Someone's broken his spirit."

The man said a boy's spirits were not so easily broken, and the signora replied that she did not think it had been done easily, but they had succeeded in the end.

The man thought she ought to do something about it. If the child was really wretched, he said, and was wandering about by himself, it was their duty to inquire into his circumstances and help him. But the signora only said, "What can one do to help a broken heart? And as for his circumstances, I've no right to interfere. He could be given money so that he could go by train to join his circus and wouldn't have to walk, but neither you nor I have any money to spare, Pierre, and it won't do the boy any harm to walk. Anyway, I gather he thumbs lifts most of the way. That's what they generally do these days."

When the stranger had gone, David went downstairs and found the signora had breakfast ready for him. Then he sat for her again, and while they were resting after lunch, she said he could look through her books.

He did not settle down to reading anything, however. There was a large photograph album on the bookcase. There were photographs from many countries, and some of them had the names of the places written underneath. There were photographs of people as well, and in many of them he could recognize the signora. Some of the pictures lay loosely in the album, and from the back of the book one bigger than the rest fell out.

David did not know how long he had been sitting with it in his hand when the signora came in.

"Who's that?" he asked when he saw her, and he showed her the photograph.

"That's a friend of mine. She's called Edith Hjort Fengel."

"Will you tell me about her?"

"What for?"

"Because her eyes look as if . . . as if she'd known a great deal, and yet she's still smiling."

"You're a sharp boy, David. Her story's mostly a sad one. She lived abroad with her husband in a country where . . . where the political situation made it necessary to be very careful. And her husband wasn't . . . One night the police arrested them— all three of them, her husband, herself, and their little boy, who was then only a year old. He was the one who was called David, just like you, and whom I never saw . . . They killed her husband and the child, and Edith only got away because one of her guards was in love with her. He got papers for her and smuggled her across the frontier, and now she lives in Denmark and is as . . . well, as well as you can be when you've once been through great un- happiness. All suffering has an end, David, if only you wait long enough. Try to remember that . . . Sorrow has its life just like people. Sorrow is born and lives and dies. And when it's dead and gone, someone's left behind to remember it. Exactly like people."

7

The wind was blowing icy cold, and the snow was falling so thickly that David could not see his hand in front of him. He knew he had very little strength left, and yet he struggled on step by step. He was determined not to die. He would go on and on until he came to Denmark and found the woman who must be his mother. He would let nothing stand in his way now. Neither snow nor cold nor mountains would stop him. He was David, a boy on the run, but one who now knew where he was going.

The day before, he had had a lift in a car from Lugano. But when they reached a place called Faido, the driver would not go any farther. The weather was bad, he said, and the pass would be closed. David had slept in a stable outside of the town, and that morning he had trudged on, the road climbing up and up and the air growing colder and colder until at last the snow came.

The Danish woman had told him he could come back to her when she returned from Rome. She had said if there were any way in which she could help him, he must ask her, and she had added that if he did not care for the circus and had no near relatives to go to, she would be pleased to have him live with her. But David had only half listened to what she was saying.

Fortunately, he was well used to hiding his thoughts and feelings. He had answered politely and remembered to thank her and had behaved just as if nothing had happened. And he had told her he had an uncle in the circus who was very nice to him. He told her all the lies he could lay tongue to, and he no longer felt it was wrong. He had to get to Denmark, and he would have to lie himself out of any situation that stood in his way or might put *them* on his tracks. Hadn't the Frenchman talked about investigating his circumstances? Nothing and no one should stop him now. Yet he knew himself that the Danish signora would have understood if he could have told her.

He had asked her the name of the camp guard, and it was the man. David understood everything now . . . or nearly everything. The man had saved the woman's life because he liked her, in the way grown-up people liked those they wanted to marry.

He had not saved her husband because he hated him for being her husband. He had saved David's life because he was her child. He had not told her the child was still alive, however, perhaps because he could only get papers for one, though David did not think that could be the whole reason. *They* always wanted revenge . . . Because the woman did not care for him, the man had gotten his revenge by turning David into a boy from a concentration camp . . . Yes . . . that's how it was. And yet the man had seen to it that he did not die. He had given him milk and vitamins and had always insisted that "the boy knows nothing."

David began to understand a lot of things now . . . *They* had let Johannes starve and freeze and made him work, even when he fell ill, but apart from that they had not ill-treated him as they had the other prisoners. And David had believed that they could not lay hands on Johannes when he looked them straight in the eye. But he now saw that that was not the only thing—the man had seen to it that Johannes should be there to look after David.

Johannes said that the older one grew, the more complicated and involved one's feelings became, and sometimes they were quite opposed to one another, as, for example, when you would like to stay awake but felt you wanted to fall asleep (at the same time). That was how the man had felt . . . He had hated David because of his mother who would have nothing to do with him, and at the same time he had looked after him, also because of his mother. And in the end he had let him escape.

That was how David himself felt, too. He hated the man, both because he was bad and because he had made him into a boy who seemed odd to other people and would never be able to shake himself entirely free of the concentration camp. Yet at the same time David could not hate him wholeheartedly because in the end he had let him go.

No one had bribed the man . . . There was no one to do it since nobody knew of David's existence. And if you knew anything about *them*, then you knew, too, the danger the man had risked in letting a prisoner escape—and yet he had done it.

David's steps grew slower and slower. He had lost all feeling in his feet now, and he was cold to the bone. The snow continued falling. He felt an irresistible urge to lie down, if only for a moment. But he dared not give way—he might die of cold out in the snow. He could no longer follow the road . . . Everything was covered with snow, and he could see nothing at all through the thickly falling flakes. There had not been a signpost for a long time.

At last his mind grew numb, and as on the road to Salonika, his feet carried him along quite unconsciously.

Suddenly there was nowhere in front of him to set the foot that was about to take the next step forward. David threw himself backward, fell, and rolled over. A precipice! He had nearly walked over the edge! Before he had become so exhausted that he just let his feet carry him along of their own accord, he had been well aware of the danger. Before the snow had begun falling, he had seen how easy it was to miss one's footing and go hurtling down the mountainside.

He would have to think what he was doing . . . Not for one second could he afford to relax his attention. He no longer dared to walk, and so he crawled onward on all fours, feeling his way carefully with his hands to make sure he was not near the edge of the precipice.

He did not know how many hours passed in this way. He ached all over, and the snow continued to swirl about him in a howling gale that seemed to cut right into his head. He was blinded and deafened, and the pain of his aching body grew so intense that he felt he could not last another minute. It was worse than anything he could think of—worse than the camp, worse even than *them*. And he could not call on God to help him, for the words were blown away inside his head, swept away into the howling gale and the blinding white hell all around him.

There was no way out but to die. David struck his head against something hard. He fell, and then it snowed no more. A voice cried, "What kind of young thief's this staggering about in this sort of weather!" With difficulty David opened his eyes sufficiently to realize he had come across one of *them*.

Then he knew no more.

That winter was the longest David had ever experienced.

The farmer was an evil-hearted man. David had escaped from the wind and the snow only to be treated like a prisoner in this man's house. It was the stable door he had struck his head against, and that stable became his shelter for the winter—and not very good shelter either. All day long he had to work and slave as hard as he could, and a bit harder if possible. The farmer was just like one of *them*. He used threats to force David to work and said he would hand him over to the police if he did not obey.

David had now learned how the members of a family spoke to one another, pleasantly and smilingly, but there was nothing like that here. The farmer was cold and brutal even to his wife and two children, but David could not feel any particular sympathy for them, for the wife was a clumsy, silent woman with a sharp edge to her tongue, and as for the children—David had never thought it possible for anyone who was still a child to be so bad. The boy was the younger, and he looked just like his father. He had stiff, unattractive straw-colored hair and very pale blue eyes, and when he played, it was always the same story—he either destroyed something or got into mischief. Whenever he had a chance, he was cruel to the animals, but he knew he would get a beating if he was found out—not that the farmer had anything against violence as such, but the animals were worth money and so they must not be ill-treated. Yet the boy could not keep his hands off them; his greatest pleasure was causing pain to a living creature.

Johannes had once said that violence and cruelty were just a stupid person's way of making himself felt, because it was easier to use your hands to strike a blow than to use your brain to find a logical and just solution to a problem.

Nevertheless, it made David feel sick to see the boy's cruelty. And the girl was not much better. True, she was not cruel to the beasts, but she was not kind either. When David considered that she was about the same age as Maria, he was shocked at the difference between them. There was Maria, like a flower in the grace of her movements, with a laugh like the tinkle of slender polished glasses touching together, Maria with her ready smile, full of affection that she lavished on everyone, grownups, children, animals—even on a runaway boy.

And then this girl who did nothing to please anyone—not even her own mother!

They all treated David like a dog . . . They threw his food to him and called him names, but they did not lay hands on him. They had left him lying in the stable until he had recovered, and then they had put him to work. But when, during one of the first days he spent there, the farmer had been about to strike him, his wife had told him to let the boy be. She had said, "You're always so stupid, Hans! He can work—I'll not meddle with that—and the stable's good enough for him. A young thief like him knows which side his bread's buttered, and he'll not make a fuss about that. But if you lay hands on him, he'll murder us all in our beds—you can tell by the look of him! And the youngsters'd do well to keep out of his way if they don't want to get beaten up, that you may be sure of! You've got free labor for the winter, and that'll have to do. Then we can hand him over to the police in the spring."

David thought they were all stupid—wicked, but stupid as well. If they had touched him, he would have been forced to go out into the snow again and freeze to death, but he would never have used physical violence against them. He hated them, and he would rather have let himself be killed than be like them.

In a way it was amusing. Yes, "amusing" was the right word . . . Apart from hitting him, they intended to see to it that life was made as wretched for him as they could make it, and yet it was still to his advantage!

He knew now that he could never have lasted through the winter tramping the roads . . . He would have died of hunger and cold. At least he had shelter where he was, and food every day.

The stable was cold, and sometimes the snow was blown into drifts until it lay as high as the roof outside. But as it hardened, the stable grew warmer inside, and the animals added a little to the warmth.

He was not given much food, only dry bread or cold scraps, and yet he had more to eat than he had been used to in the camp, and it tasted no worse—sometimes, in fact, a little better.

They thought they were making him suffer by leaving him to sleep alone in the dark stable, but night was his pleasantest time!

David was not afraid of the dark. There were only common everyday objects about him, and the animals asleep. It seemed quite natural. The darkness altered nothing, and David was not frightened of it. What he was afraid of was people.

At nighttime the stable was his. In the camp he had never been alone, and David liked to be left by himself to think in peace.

Then the dog came.

David had always thought of dogs as enemies—*their* tools. It was one of their pastimes to make the dogs bite the prisoners. Since his escape into Italy, he had of course noticed that good people kept dogs, too, but he had always given them a wide berth, just in case they could tell where he came from, and then they *would* bite him.

But shut up in the stable, he could not avoid the dog. It came one night when it was snowing hard and a gale was howling outside. David lay quite still and much against his will let it sniff all around him. The farmer and his family spoke a peculiar kind of German; perhaps that was the reason David spoke to it in Italian.

"I'm afraid of you," he said softly, in as steady a voice as he could muster. "You're sure to notice I come from the camp, and then you'll bite me. And there's nothing I can do about it." David could see the dog as it went on sniffing around him like a big black shadow against the darkness. Then it lay down by his side, pushing and turning until they were lying back to back. It yawned very loudly, and David felt its warm moist breath. Then it gave a sigh and fell asleep.

It did not bite him, and David was not nearly so cold in the night, for the dog was big and kept him warm. It was called King.

It often growled at the farmer's children, and David knew it was not very fond of the farmer, either, though he rarely struck it—no doubt because it was a good sheepdog, and in the summer, when the animals were out to graze, he could not do without it.

But whenever it saw David, it would wag its tail, and it went to sleep with him every night.

David gradually began to grow fond of it. One evening as he lay awake wondering if the winter would ever come to an end, he held his hand out to the dog when it came to lie down beside him. He did it without thinking. Perhaps he had missed it and wanted it to come and share its warmth with him. He found himself touching its head, feeling the roundness of its skull under his hand, and liking the firm warm feel of it. The dog did not move, and David let his hand glide slowly over the dog's thick coat, just once.

Then he took his hand away and lay still again.

The dog lifted its head and turned toward him, and David felt its warm wet tongue carefully licking his hand.

And so David and the dog became friends.

But David was beginning to grow impatient. It seemed as if that winter would go on forever, and he wanted to be up and on his way, on and on until he came to Denmark, where he would try to find the woman who had changed everything, so that he was no longer just a boy wandering aimlessly and always appearing strange to other people, but one who knew where he was going.

When he found her, he might perhaps learn not to seem strange and different . . . and to do it in such a way that he would still be himself. He tried to avoid taking it for granted that she would be glad he was still alive, for he obviously could not be sure she would. Since she had always assumed he was dead, she might find it difficult to get used to the idea that he was David, especially when he was so different from other boys and knew so little of the world outside the concentration camp.

But he was sure from her photograph that she would be a good woman, and clever, too. She would tell him what to do to avoid causing suspicion until he was sufficiently grown up for it not to matter anymore if he chose to go his own way. Perhaps she would be able to find somewhere where he could work with kind, goodhearted people.

He found it difficult not to let his thoughts run away with him! Now and then he would find himself in the middle of a wonderful, happy daydream where he would fancy she would be glad . . . she would see at once that he was David and would want to love him just as the children's father and mother loved the children in the house. Then he would come to the end of his wanderings. He would have a place where he belonged and would be able to ask about all the things he did not know and learn all he wanted to. She would say "my son" when she spoke of him, and he would never have to be afraid again. And as his thoughts ran on, he would tell himself that she was surrounded with fine things, understood music, and loved and appreciated beauty. He thought of all the things he would be able to tell her. He would not want to say anything about the most dreadful things he had seen, but he would be able to talk about Johannes and all that he had seen and learned since his escape. And about Maria and all the things he had thought of. It would be like staying with Signora Hartmann—only much, much better, for now he would belong.

There was a king in Denmark, too—it was a

free country. If it all turned out like that, there was nothing he could think of good enough to do in return for the God of the green pastures and still waters.

But it would not be quite like that, not quite so wonderful, probably. It would be good, though, and David longed for the winter to pass so that he could be on his way again.

Then one morning the sun crept into the stable through a tiny little window high up under the roof, a window that had been covered with thick frost all the time he had been with the farmer.

David's heart began to beat faster. As he lay there perfectly still, he had the impression that if he moved, that weak little ray of sunshine might disappear. He had not seen the sun for such a long time that he had almost forgotten its existence. It did not reach down to where he lay, and so he got up and slowly stretched his arms toward it.

If he stretched as high as he could, he might just be able to touch the pale little beam of light with his hand. Suddenly it was the most important thing in the world to reach up to the sunlight, but however hard he stretched, the sun would not reach farther than the tips of his fingers.

David decided he would see if he could find something to do on the other side of the house that looked down into the valley, but the farmer was near him all the time, and he was not able to see anything.

And that evening as he lay awake, he heard the farmer push the great bar into place across the stable door!

Then David knew that spring was on the way. It would come first to the valley below, and that was why the farmer had taken good care that David should have no opportunity of looking down there that day; he did not want him to see the signs of spring. Later it would come to the mountain pastures. David worked hard every day, and so the farmer would keep him imprisoned there as long as he could. And when he could no longer hide the fact that spring had come and there was no more snow to help him guard David, he would call in the police. That would be the end. *They* would come and take him back to the camp.

David stared into the darkness. He would never get away, never. The bar was as thick as a tree trunk, and it would take him many, many nights to hack through it with his knife. And the farmer would see where he had worked at it the very first morning.

"God of the green pastures and still waters, why have You done it?" asked David. "What have I done wrong? I rescued Maria from the fire and saved her life so that I could thank You . . . And all through this long winter I haven't once caused You any trouble, though I have sometimes thought they were bad people you brought me to. But I haven't complained, and I haven't asked You to make it better, though I've got two lots of help left over from that time with Maria . . . You must know the farmer and his family are bad people, and I hate them. And I thought perhaps it was You who got Signora Hartmann to paint me so that I could find the picture of the woman who was my mother. I chose You, and I can't alter that now, but I want You to know that I think You're cruel, just like the farmer here and Carlo and all that belong to them. And I suppose You'll never help me again, even if I do have some help still to come, because You're tired of me. I'm sorry I didn't choose a better God. I am David. Amen."

David felt a little better now. It was good to get it off his chest. Then he began to feel frightened. Suppose God grew terribly angry when He was criticized! Suppose He kept hostages just as *they* did . . . Then some harm might befall Maria. He couldn't do very much to David but let him die. Oh, yes, worse than that; He could let him be taken back to the camp and make him live there. But it would be worse still if He did anything to Maria.

But it *was* true He was cruel. David had waited patiently all the winter and put up with things without complaining and whimpering. And then God let the farmer bar the door, and it was only at nighttime that David could get away.

David wasted two precious nights before he realized where the trouble lay.

And he might have known right away, for Johannes had once told him. They had heard one of the guards put the blame for some neglect of duty on another who had retorted that it was the fault of a third man, and Johannes had said to David, "Never let me hear you say it's someone else's fault. It often is, but you must never shirk your own responsibility. There's always something where you're at fault, too, and that fault you must discover and learn to recognize and take the consequences of it . . . both because it's the only honorable thing to do and also because it's the easier way. You can't change others, but you can do something about a fault in yourself."

He had told God plainly what the fault was! He had said God was cruel like Carlo and the farmer and all bad people, when perhaps God just wanted to teach him where his own fault lay! He had been cruel himself. He was not the only one who had waited patiently without complaining. Carlo had, too . . . and David had taken no notice. Carlo had said he was sorry, several times, and David had refused to forgive him for being bad. But suppose Carlo was not really bad, suppose he were only rather stupid . . . He had never tried to get even because David would not talk to him while he was in the house. On the contrary, the children's mother had told their father that Carlo had done his utmost to be good friends with David and had been very upset when David would not respond.

David sat up in the dark. He must get away from here . . . There must be some way, and he would have to find it. He remembered the address of the house. He could write a letter and buy a stamp. If he let himself remain a prisoner, Carlo would never get to know that David had discovered he was not perhaps really bad at all but only stupid.

The door was impossible, and the window was too small . . .

But if spring were not in too great a hurry to come up the mountainside, then he might be able to take advantage of the snow! He could cut a hole in the stable wall, in the end farthest from the house, so that no one would hear him at work . . . and then dig a tunnel through the snow, which lay piled up to the roof, and so get out that way, some distance from the house!

During the days that followed, David was so sleepy in the daytime that he made a mess of everything. He had to stay awake all night in order to get on with his plan! Fortunately, the stable was a wooden building. His knife grew blunter and blunter, but at last he managed to hack out a big square hole large enough to get through.

He replaced the loose boards every morning and put a bucket in front of them so that the farmer should not discover the hole. Then he began digging out the snow. The bucket came in handy, and he emptied the snow he dug out into the beasts' drinking trough. David thought what a good thing it was the farmer was so stupid or he would certainly have wondered why the animals were no longer thirsty! However, it was a bigger job than David had imagined, and he had to get a little sleep every night. He was very much afraid spring would come too early and the snow begin to thaw, perhaps even collapse on top of him in the tunnel. He was also afraid that in the end the farmer would begin to ask himself why David was so sleepy in the daytime instead of just grumbling at him.

He still kept his hands off him. One day he was just going to strike him but stopped abruptly when the dog placed himself in front of David and stood there growling. David was puzzled, but when he realized the dog was ready to protect him against the farmer, he went into the stable and cried. He had no idea why, but he seemed overcome by the thought that a creature wanted to protect him, although he had done nothing to deserve it.

That very evening David overheard the farmer tell his wife that the youngster would have to be handed over to the police right away because he had gotten a hold on the dog.

What silly wicked nonsense, David thought angrily. He had never never had a hold over anybody, or ever wanted to have. And if he ever got such a hold, without being able to help it, he would not make use of it. A hold over others, brute force, violence—that was all *they* ever thought of.

He would have to get away that night.

The tunnel was twice his own length. He did not know if it were long enough, but it would have to do—he had no more time. When it was dark and the farmer and his family were at supper, David slipped out and thrust a long broomstick through the snow behind the stable just where he reckoned the tunnel ended. Half the broomstick stuck out of the snow!

That meant he would be able to get through that night. But it also meant that if the farmer spotted the stick, he would undoubtedly guess what David was up to.

David waited with beating heart for the farmer's footsteps when he came to bar the door. Would he take a walk around now that it was no longer snow-ing?

But the farmer went straight in again—it was still very cold out.

David fought down his feeling of nausea; he always felt like being sick when he had been most frightened. But that night he had no time to stop. He *wouldn't* be sick, but he was in spite of that.

The dog was uneasy that evening. First it lay watching him as he worked at the tunnel, its eyes shining in the dark, and then it tried to help him with the digging, trotting backward and forward and scrabbling in the snow just where David was going to put the bucket. After a bit he got the idea of placing both its forepaws on the bucket and pushing so that it bit into the snow more easily. It whined a little now and then and followed David with its eyes while he was looking for his bundle and packing his things together. Fortunately, there had been nothing in it the farmer could find a use for! He had gone through it and thrown it back to David when he had seen what was in it.

David tidied himself up as well as he could in the darkness and carefully disentangled Maria's cross, which he had tied firmly inside the belt of his trou-sers so that he should not lose it. As he fastened the chain around his neck, he said softly to the dog,

"I must go now. Thank you for keeping me so warm at night, King, but most of all for wanting to protect me against *them*. I've never known what it was like before for someone to want to protect me. Good-bye."

He took a firm hold of the dog's thick warm neck and laid his head against it, and King licked him enthusiastically around the chin.

Then David crawled into the tunnel until he came to the hole he had made by wriggling the broomstick around. The dog followed him, but David said, "No, King. You must stay here where you get food every day. Good-bye."

And so he was out in the open. It was still very, very cold. By listening to the conversation of the farmer and his wife, he had found out how to get down to the road that wound on through the mountains, and perhaps it would not be quite so cold farther down, now that spring was on its way. It was already April.

David hurried along as fast as he dared. The night was still and clear enough for him to see where he was going. An hour passed in half scrambling, half walking down to where the road should be, and then he saw it.

Men had begun to clear it to make a way through the snow, but it would be some time yet before a car could drive along it. David was able to walk in the cleared part without too much difficulty. And the going would soon be easier, for he knew he was high up in the neighborhood of a pass called the St. Gotthard, and farther down spring would be more advanced.

He looked back over his shoulder at the white mountain. Winter had come to an end at last . . . and he had his freedom once more. He was glad he had discovered the meaning of the barred door. Everything had gone smoothly since then. Yes, he had made a good choice after all when he had chosen the God of the green pastures and the still waters! He was very powerful, and the fact that He expected you to think for yourself and do something in return for His help did not matter, as long as you could work things out.

David did not know how long he had been aware of the dark dot up on the mountainside. It was moving toward him. He was not yet free! He turned and ran . . . The moon was shining now. If he could reach the turn of the road where it swept around a spur of rock, he might be able to dig himself into the snow before the farmer arrived on the scene . . .

David never knew how he managed to do it. Everything went black in front of his eyes as he lay in the snow.

Then a warm wet feeling on his face woke him up.

It was not the farmer after all! It was the dog who wanted to go with him!

It trotted along by his side, sometimes running on ahead but always returning to keep him company, and every time he spoke to it, it would wag its tail.

David breathed deeply, hardly noticing the cold bite in the air. He was David. He was free and strong. He was on the move again, but this time he knew where he was making for. There might be many difficulties ahead before he reached his goal, but difficulties could be overcome. He still had one more promise of help left over from God, and he had the dog who was going with him of its own free will. The long winter had passed, and he was going down to meet the spring.

8

The spring was beautiful. It was still cold the first night he had to spend out, but he found a stable, and he and the dog slept close together. The next day spring had really arrived. He had some difficulty with his money . . . He still had a little money with him from Italy, and he had not spent it before winter overtook him and he found himself a prisoner at the farm. But when he went into a shop, he was told that his money was no good in Switzerland, and he would have to take it to a bank. He had been afraid to go . . . for suppose the farmer had put the police onto him . . . but he had gone nevertheless, for he had to have bread and King was not used to being so hungry.

But he had also managed to earn some money that he could use in Switzerland. He had been lucky, for it was not easy to get work among the

Swiss—often they all looked dour, as if they never laughed.

Their country was very beautiful. The sun shone upon the white snowcaps of the great mountain peaks and turned them to a glowing pink. In the valleys the grass was a startling green, and the houses were surrounded by trees covered in white and pink blossoms. The first time David saw them, he found himself smiling.

The delicate blossoms brought Maria to mind. A tree in full bloom was among the most beautiful of all things, and David's smile came unbidden. Yes, it was good to be alive.

When he had provided himself with money he could use, he bought a stamp and an envelope. The letter was not very neat, for he had written it sitting on the grass with the pad on his knee. But he would not feel easy in his mind until it was done—he did not want God to think he had forgotten the lesson of the barred door!

So David wrote:

"To Carlo.

"Carlo, I want you to know I'm no longer so sure you're bad. Perhaps you're only stupid. And so I'll stop hating you, because I only hate those that are bad. But if you ever use force again and

I get to know about it, then I shall hate you again. Will you thank your parents for writing the letter in the paper. I saw it. And will you say I've written to you. Tell your parents and Andrea and the two little ones and Maria. Tell Maria first, and tell her I've seen a tree full of bloom that's made me think of her again.

"David"

He wrote "Carlo" on the envelope, and then the children's father's full name and the name of the town near where the house lay and last of all "Italy." He had made quite sure Carlo would get the letter. It took him some time to find out what a mailbox looked like in Switzerland, but he finally succeeded.

Everything went splendidly . . . For a whole day David walked along the side of a lake that lay greener than the greenest tree among the high mountains. David enjoyed the walk so much that he did not bother with a lift. But perhaps there was another reason, too, for he did not feel quite at ease with the Swiss—they did not look so friendly as the Italians. And all the tourist traffic was going in the opposite direction.

Railway stations, he had found, had a further advantage besides offering a chance to earn money; there was often a map there that he could look at.

He knew he had to keep to the north, but apart from that, he had only a rough idea of the route he must follow.

He managed to earn some money at the station in Lucerne. He had to spend more, now that he had the dog with him, for it ate a lot, and he hoped there would soon be tourists traveling northward. He had come to a city called Basle. It was somewhat out of his way, but he had noticed in Lucerne that Basle lay partly in France . . . the France Johannes had come from . . . a place called Alsace. And although he wanted to get on as fast as possible, he thought he must stop to look at it.

But he found he would have to cross a great river to get to France, and the frontier ran along it through the town. There was a road barrier and soldiers and passports to be inspected—and so David did not go into Alsace.

Instead he accepted a lift in a Swiss truck after all. He left Basle along the road that was signposted to Germany. The great lofty snowcapped peaks had been left behind now, and the mountains had become round and green and much less high. But the countryside was still beautiful, and David liked the look of the houses. They were quite different from those in Italy; they were not as picturesque, but they were very, very clean, and they looked attractive with their window boxes full of flowers. After he left the truck, he soon found himself at another frontier post. There were police about, but there were only a couple of them, and they were busily examining a man's papers—a tall man from Switzerland driving a big truck. So David turned off the narrow road, and when he was out of sight, he ran up the hillside and back to the road on the other side of the barrier, into Germany.

But he had not been walking more than a minute or two when a truck pulled up in front of him, the one he had just seen at the frontier post! David was frightened. He had not looked at the man closely . . . Perhaps he was one of *them* . . . Why else should he have stopped?

King seemed to sense his fear; the dog placed itself in front of him and growled at the man.

"Well, my little vagabond, you slipped across that frontier pretty nimbly, eh?"

King stopped growling, and David looked up quickly into the man's face. You could hardly say he looked as if he were in the habit of laughing; on the contrary, he looked worried and depressed, but kind and friendly, too. Perhaps it was because his face was lined in a peculiar way that he looked so sad.

"Yes," said David. What else could he say?

"Hm. Where are you going to, then?"

"Brunswick."

"Well, I'm not going as far as that, but I can give you a lift to Frankfurt if your dog can make himself at home in the truck . . ."

David thanked him and said he thought King would sit still but he did not know for sure, and the Swiss driver smiled and said he was honest, at any rate.

David felt uncomfortable. That was the worst part of it; he wanted to be honest, but he was always driven to telling lies. People questioned him, and then he had to fall back upon the story he had invented. The only point he was quite frank about was his name, for he *was* David, and that was something he would always stand by. The Swiss truck driver was called Graf, and David hated telling him all about the circus and being taken ill in Naples. It went against the grain to lie to someone who seemed so kind and gentle in his manner.

David thought the food he gave him quite delicious, and King got something to eat, too, and when they reached Frankfurt (it would have taken David a good many days to do the journey on foot), the man gave David some money—five of the coins they used in Germany—marks they were called.

"I'm not sure you aren't a little rascal," the man

said. "But you've a clear look in your eye and your dog loves you, so you must be a good boy, whatever you are. You haven't run away from your parents, have you? The truth, David!"

David looked him straight in the face. "No, I haven't run away from my parents. That's the truth," he added quickly. "And thank you for giving me and my dog food and for driving us such a long way."

The Swiss stood watching him until he reached the corner of the street. Then he raised his hand and waved. Hesitantly David raised his own and waved back . . . somewhat awkwardly, for he had never waved to anyone before.

During the days that followed David got several lifts, and King learned to lie perfectly still across David's feet so that no one could accuse him of being restless. People were always nervous about him at first, for he often looked as if he would bite, and he *was* very big. But when they saw how meekly he did everything David told him to, they would laugh and call him a sheep in wolf's clothing . . . for David always spoke very quietly and politely to him in a way they obviously did not think it possible to talk to a dog. But David did not mind. King had chosen to go with him, and so he was not going to show ingratitude by ordering him about . . . David hated orders himself and loud commanding voices, and as long as King was with him, he would remain a free dog.

He was a clever dog, too. David had heard people say a dog was "as clever as a human being," but that, he thought, was nonsense. A dog was a dog, and a man was a man, and you could not be as clever as something quite different. But a dog could certainly be clever in a doggy sort of way, and King was clever—and good.

Everything had gone well since he gave the farmer the slip and the dog joined him. There had been times, of course, when he was hungry and felt the cold . . . but nothing had happened to frighten him. He had not seen anyone who looked like *them*, and he knew where he was going.

It was comforting to have King with him. He could not carry on a conversation with King, naturally, but it was good to know the dog was there, keeping him warm at night and always ready to protect him. David knew he could not rely too much on the dog's protection, for though it could bite, it could not get the better of a man—not one of *them*, at any rate; they always went armed. But it was a comfort just to know it wanted to protect him.

David was to learn his mistake.

Perhaps it happened because he was in too much of a hurry. He was able to plan his route from the maps he found in railway stations, and he had become quite good at working out how long a particular stretch of the journey would take if he got a lift or if he had to walk. He knew that it would not take him many days now to reach Denmark. Perhaps it happened, too, because for hours at a time he could now forget his fears—almost, but not quite. He had had fear too well drilled into him for him ever to be completely free of it. But it was not so bad now, for now he was sure the man really had intended him to get to Denmark. There had been no trap. And the children's parents had not given him away either. There was only the farmer, and David thought he was too stupid to imagine David might have run away from *them*.

A search was being made for him, of course; the man's influence was limited, and he would not have been able to prevent it. But no one knew *where* to look for him. And now Denmark was almost within reach . . . Denmark and the woman who was his mother.

He must have been walking for half an hour before he was suddenly aware of his fear and knew he should have sensed danger earlier. It was dusk, and he had been too preoccupied with finding a good place to sleep.

He knew at once that something was wrong. That building farther down the hillside . . . and the men standing idly about . . .

He called to King softly, in a whisper.

He had returned to *them*!

He lay as still as death behind a bush. It was lucky King always did as he was told and was now also lying perfectly still by his side. David's thoughts ran on . . . How had it happened? There was no doubt about it; he was back among *them*. David knew the signs. He was only too familiar with the way *they* looked. It must have happened when the dog ran off over the fields. David would sometimes play with the dog. It would run off with a stone or a stick in its mouth, intending David to chase it. David thought it was rather pointless, really, and not very amusing, but the dog liked it, and so David would join in to please it.

But he ought to have known something was wrong as soon as they had got back to the road, and now that he thought of it, he realized the three people they had met on the way should have aroused his suspicions. People always looked like that where *they* were—like prisoners in a concentration camp, weary, gray-faced, apprehensive . . . dejected and sorrowful, as though they had forgotten life could be good . . . dull-eyed and apathetic, as if they no longer thought about anything.

The dog looked at him questioningly and began quietly whimpering. David placed his hand over its muzzle and it stopped, but it continued to look at him. The bush was too thin, its new green leaves too small. David quite forgot how beautiful he had thought spring was only that morning, with its small new bright-green leaves. His one thought now was that anyone could look through the bush and see him lying on the ground—and he was David, the boy who had fled from *them.*

In their barracks they would have a list of everybody who was under suspicion and should be arrested on sight. *Their* guards always had a list like that. On that list would be found: "David. A thin boy with brown hair, escaped from concentration camp." And under the heading "Recognition Marks" would be: "It is obvious from the appearance of his eyes that he is not an ordinary boy but only a prisoner."

If the men had not been talking so loudly, they would have heard him already . . . They were much too close to him, and he would never be able to get away. Even if he waited until it was quite dark, they would hear him as soon as he moved.

His flight would end where it began—at the point of a rifle, for he would not stop when they shouted to him. If he stopped, they would not shoot, but they would interrogate him instead and send him back to the camp. And there, strong and healthy as he was, he would be a terribly long time dying.

No, when they called to him, he would run, and then the shot would be fired—the one that had been waiting for him ever since that night when he had walked calmly toward the tree on the way to the mine outside the camp. But this time he would not be able to walk calmly away from them. He knew now how wonderful life could be, and his desire to live would spur him on. He would run—he knew it—and it would be a victory for *them*.

David remembered all the pain and bitterness he had ever known—and how much he could remember in such a short time! He recalled, too, all the good things he had learned about since he had gained his freedom—beauty and laughter, music and kind people . . . Maria . . . and a tree smothered in pink blossom . . . a dog to walk by his side . . . and a place to aim for . . .

This would be the end of it all. David tried to

feel glad that he had known so much that was good and beautiful before the bullet found its mark, but he could not; it was too difficult. He pressed his face into the dog's long coat so that no one should hear him and wept. He wept quite quietly, but the dog grew uneasy and wanted to whimper again.

David stopped crying. "God," he whispered, "God of the green pastures and the still waters, I've one promise of help left, but it's too late now. You can't do anything about this. I don't mean to be rude, because I know You're very strong and You could make those men down there want to walk away for a bit. But they won't. They don't know You, You see, and they're not afraid of You. But they are afraid of the commandant because he'll have them shot if they leave their posts. So You can see there's nothing You can do now. But please don't think I'm blaming You. It was my own fault for not seeing the danger in time. I shall run . . . Perhaps You'll see they aim straight so it doesn't hurt before I die. I'm so frightened of things that hurt. No, I forgot. I've only one promise of help left, and it's more important You should help the dog get away and find some good people to live with. Perhaps *they'll* shoot straight anyway, but if they don't, it can't be helped. You must save the dog because it once tried to protect me. Thank You for being my God; I'm glad I chose

You. And now I must run, for if I leave it any longer, I shan't have the courage to die. I am David. Amen."

The dog kept nudging him. It wanted them to go back the way they had come, away from the spot where it sensed danger lurking.

"No," David whispered, "we can't go back . . . it's too late. You must keep still, King . . . and when they've hit me, perhaps you can get away by yourself . . ."

The dog licked his cheek eagerly, impatiently nudging him again and moving restlessly as if it wanted to go on. It nudged him once more . . . and then jumped up before David could stop it.

In one swift second David understood what the dog wanted. It did not run back the way they had come . . . It was a sheepdog, and it had sensed danger . . . It was going to take David's place!

Barking loudly, it sprang toward the men . . .

"Run!" something inside him told David. "Run . . . run!" That was what the dog wanted him to do.

So he ran . . . He hesitated a moment and then ran more quickly than he had ever run in all his life. As he ran, he heard the men shouting and running, too, but in a different direction . . . One of them yelled with pain—then came the sound of a shot and a strange loud bark from the dog.

David knew the dog was dead.

He went on running. He was some distance away now, and they had not heard him. But he ran on until he had left far behind the field where they had left the road an hour before. Then he threw himself down in a ditch sobbing and gasping painfully for breath.

He felt as if he would never be able to stop crying, never. God of the pastures and waters, so strong that He could influence a person's thoughts, had let the dog run forward, although He knew it would be shot. "Oh, You shouldn't have done it!" David sobbed again and again. "The dog that followed me . . . and I was never able to look after it properly because I was only David . . . I couldn't even give it enough to eat, and it had to steal to get food . . . The dog came with me of its own free will and then had to die just because of it . . ."

Then David suddenly realized he was wrong. It was not because it had followed him that the dog was dead. The dog had gone with him freely, and it had met its death freely . . . in order to protect David from *them*. It was a sheepdog, and it knew what it was doing. It had shown David what it wanted him to do, and then it had diverted the danger from him and faced it itself . . . because it wanted to.

Its very bark as it sprang forward had seemed

to say, "Run, run!" And all the while David was running, he had known he must not turn back and try to save it. He must not let the dog's action be in vain; he had to accept it.

Had God of the green pastures and the still waters entered into the dog and made it do it, or had it just done it because it wanted to? Oh, but he never wanted anyone to suffer for his sake . . . and the dog had given its life . . . and he had never been able to do anything for it. So one could get something for nothing after all?

David stood still in the big city and looked around him.

On shop signs and posters were words not altogether unfamiliar to him, but by and large the language was quite strange. "Denmark," he told himself. "I'm in Denmark."

He scarcely knew how he came to be there. Since the night he had realized that the dog had died for him, he felt as if nothing had really penetrated his thoughts.

He had gotten lifts most of the way, and the drivers had shared their food with him. They were all concerned about him and remarked how ill he looked. He had felt better sitting in a truck. All the time he was walking, he thought he could see the dog running along just in front of him, although he knew it could not be true.

He had met several Danish truck drivers in Germany, all quiet men with little to say, and they had all been kind to him.

And he had come to Denmark. He had come straight across the frontier with one of them . . . He had been traveling in a big truck, and the driver had stowed him away inside. He had told him it was against the law, but he said he had boys of his own at home, and he could not bring himself to hand David over to the customs officers in the state he was in. He said the officers would be kind enough to him, but there would be no end of paperwork to go through, and what David needed was to get to the family he spoke about as quickly as possible and get into a good warm bed.

In a town called Kolding the truck driver had gotten hold of a friend who, he said, would take David on to Copenhagen. David had begun to pick up a little of the language. The two men had said something about "Passport or no passport, a bit of a lad like him can't have anything serious against him, and you can see with half an eye he can't hold out much longer."

David had watched the countryside passing by. There were no mountains, no big rivers. Everything was small and compact. But bright and cheerful, too—the houses, the people, the woods, everything. David had never imagined woods could look like these, their coloring bright and delicate like sunshine on one of Maria's dresses. There was beauty in Denmark, too, but beauty of a different kind. But all the while he felt too tired to look at it properly.

He had been on a ship, too . . . The driver bought him a ticket, and so he did not even have to hide. But when they came to the big city called Copenhagen, David tried to pull himself together. The driver said if David could just give him the address, he would put him down at the right place.

But he could not, of course. He had told the driver it was in his bundle in the back of the truck. It was not the truth, and when the man realized he had no address, he would be suspicious. David knew by this time that nothing very serious would happen to him here, because it was a free country, but you could not be too careful . . . If they found a strange boy with nowhere to go, they might consider it their duty to hand him over to the police, especially if he were not Danish. One thing David had really gotten into his head during all the days that had passed since the dog's death—he must reach the woman in Denmark, for if it should turn out that the dog had given its life for him and all to no purpose, it would be too awful to think about, as if the dog's sacrifice had been despised. And that must never be.

David had watched the driver make a telephone call. He had gone into a little glassed-in box affair, and there were books where you could find the numbers you wanted to call and people's addresses. He only had to slip away while the driver was not looking and find another telephone kiosk.

They pulled up on a large square, and the driver said something to him that David pretended not to understand. The man was going to buy what he called a "hot dog" to give him. As soon as he left the truck, David dropped to the ground on the other side. He quickly ran to the back of the truck, opened it, and snatched up his bundle. There were crowds of people, and it was easy enough to hide among them.

It was hardly the thing to do when the driver had been so kind to him, but there was no other way out. David felt as certain as if he had been told that he would very soon come to the end of his strength, and before that happened, he must try to find the woman.

He ran along street after street, turning corners all the time, until he felt safe. He had no difficulty in finding a telephone kiosk, and there were the directories all in order!

He found six people called Hjort Fengel, but there was only one with an "E" in front of the name. And the address was Strandvejen 758.

It must be a long street, and David decided to ask . . . There were many people who could understand you if you spoke English. He stood there for a moment or two with the book in his hand and looked about him. But before he could make up his mind whom to ask, a woman spoke to him. She asked if she could help him in any way. David answered politely in English, and she understood what he said.

She told him the address was a very long way off. Then she looked at him and said, "But I'm going that way myself. I can take you most of the way in the car . . ."

She asked him what country he came from, and David told her he was French, since he could not very well say he came from nowhere at all. She seemed to realize he was tired, for after that she said very little, and David sat looking out of the window. Soon they came to the sea, and David thought it was almost as blue as it was in Italy, where he had made his home among the rocks. That seemed a very long time ago now, and he found it difficult to remember so far back.

David stood for a long time looking at number

758. Everything smelled fresh and pleasant. There were trees everywhere with white and yellow and lilac-colored blossoms. The sun was shining, the leaves were bright green, and the sea was a deep blue. Denmark was beautiful, too—perhaps all countries were beautiful where *they* weren't.

A few yards would take him to the door, and yet David thought he would never get there. His legs could carry him no farther, and he was on the point of collapsing. He had thought for some time that perhaps if the woman who lived there would tell him what to do next and where to go, he would be able to manage, but now he knew he couldn't. If his happiest dreams came true, he could go on living; if not, he had come to the end.

French was the language he spoke best. David picked up his bundle, walked to the door, and rang the bell, and when the woman opened it, he knew she was the woman in the photograph, the woman whose eyes had seen so much and yet could smile.

Then David said in French, "Madame . . . I am David. I am . . ."

He could say no more. The woman looked into his face and said clearly and distinctly, "David . . . my son David . . ."

About the Author

Anne Holm (1922–1998) was born in Denmark, and she began her writing career as a journalist. *I Am David* was originally published—under the title *David*—in Denmark, where it became a million-copy bestseller and received numerous awards. It was published to much acclaim in the United States as *North to Freedom*, and later was made into the movie *I Am David*. Ms. Holm said of her book, "I wrote *David* because it seemed to me that children, who can love a book more passionately than any grown person, got such a lot of harmless entertainment and not nearly enough real, valuable literature."